This one is for my husband, VANCE.

His unconditional love and support has
given me wings to fly, and helped to create the
bond and love inspired between these characters.

He is my soul mate.
My protector.
My knight in shining armor.
My one true love.

ACKNOWLEDGEMENTS

First, I have to acknowledge my editor, VICTORIA SCHMITZ
of Crimson Tide Editorial. She has been such a vital part to this
process, and I am so blessed to have her in my life. We seem to gel
amazingly well, and feed off of each other. Her jokes and crazy
stickers make the editing process a lot less daunting.

Again, I have to also thank my writing buddies and awesome
friends, CAMBRIA HEBERT and AMBER GARZA. They
inspire me daily. I would have been procrastinating a lot more
through this process if it hadn't been for their pushes and cheers.

Also, *huge* thanks to my PA, AMBER GARCIA, for working hard
to pimp my books and push me towards success.
I treasure our friendship. Love you girl!

Also, a huge thank you to my PUBLISHING FAMILY over at
Crushing Hearts and Black Butterfly. Their support has been
invaluable, and I love each and every one of them.

And last, but not least, my family. Their constant love
and support has made this dream happen.
I love you all!

I WAS
TRAPPED.
TETHERED
BETWEEN
TWO
HEARTS.

TETHERED
WINGS

ONE

HIS EYES FIXED ON MINE, and the world around me instantly faded away. The thunderous beating of my heart occupied my senses as I ascended the stairway. At the top was Kade, my bonded, the one I was supposed to spend the rest of my life with. How the hell was I going to explain everything? I could see concern on his beautiful face. He had questions, but regrettably, I didn't have the answers.

My mind was suddenly filled with thoughts of how much I missed him, and how much I missed this place.

Even though my world was filled with a constant, spiraling madness, I'd take it –and him- over Hell any day.

Hell…now *that* was an experience I wouldn't wish on my worst enemy. Well, maybe Lucian, but the bastard was already from that hellhole, so I'd just be telling him to go home.

I still couldn't wrap my head around the fact we had gone to the

Underworld. Or that, our week-long trip had totaled, four long months in the mortal world. It was no wonder they all looked at us as if we'd returned from the dead. Four months was a very long time to be missing, especially when you're on a road trip to visit with Lucifer.

As I reached Kade, every cell in my body went haywire. My pulse raced, my knees felt weak, and my hands were sweaty. It was a different feeling than when I was around Ethon, but no less exhilarating.

I hesitated. My first instinct was to run into his arms. Instead, I paused a few feet away from him, worried how things were going to play out.

His eyes were filled with confusion and relief. He was happy I was alive, but Ethon's presence threw a wrench into our delicate relationship.

I was already baffled about my Immortal Bond with Kade, and now, I had gone and bonded to the son of Lucifer. *Two bonds.* Like I didn't have enough complications?

We stood silent, the tension was thick.

"Kade," I breathed, shaking my head. I didn't know what to say or how to begin.

In a second, his eyes softened and he immediately closed the space between us. Protective arms folded around me in a warm embrace. His familiar scent enveloped me like a warm blanket. Overwhelmed with emotion, I broke.

"Hey, it's okay," he breathed. "You're safe now." He pressed his warm lips to my forehead and breathed in. Exhaling, he gently wiped away my tears. Grabbing my hand, he led me into his room, and snapped the door shut behind us. Once alone, he took me to his bed and sat me down, grabbing a chair from the far corner and placing it directly in front of me.

"I was so worried about you, Emma. From the moment I opened my eyes, I realized I wasn't with you anymore...you have no idea how much it terrified me. I wanted to be with you, but I was too damn weak. Besides, Alaine wouldn't have allowed it."

My heart ached hearing him speak those words because I had thought about him every moment I was away, too. The last time I'd seen him, he'd been so pale. I thought I would never see him again, and it had scared the hell out of me.

"I'm fine, really. Just exhausted."

"Well, when you're rested, I'd like to hear all about the adventure. I'm so proud of you. When it mattered most, you fought, and you survived."

My heart swelled as I recognized tenderness and sincerity in his eyes.

I couldn't take the compassion anymore and looked to my hands. "I promise to tell you everything, but there's one thing I really wanted to ask you. Something that's been eating away at me."

"You know you can ask me anything," he answered, lifting my chin until our eyes met again.

For a moment I was entranced by his sparkling hazel eyes. I knew I could trust him, and knew he would tell me the truth.

"I need to know why. Why did you have to give up your immortality? You said you had to become mortal to enter Hell with me, but I know that isn't true. Dominic and Malachi...they didn't have to give up anything. So, why? Was it really necessary? Help me understand."

Sadness swept over his face, and my heart shattered.

Keeping his head down, Kade slowly nodded.

"I was faced with a choice. Immortals give off a strong scent, easily detectable by other immortals. If I had escorted you into the Underworld, as an immortal, it could have cost us our lives."

Gathering confidence, he moved forward and took my face in his hands. "I had an option to minimize the risk and I took it. No regrets. And I would do it again, if it meant your safety. You've become so much more than an assignment to me, Emma. You're part of my life. I will always choose you."

Sighing, he dropped his arms and grabbed my hands.

"As for Dom and Malachi...they made their own choice."

"They went in knowing I'd risked everything to keep you safe, not wanting my decision, to become mortal, to be in vain. I would have done the same for any of them, if the situation were reversed. It's something brothers do for each other. We also have a bond, it's just different than you and I—" he hesitated, suddenly seeming helpless.

The bond between us had changed when he became mortal. The physical connection - the electrical buzz and overwhelming euphoria – was somehow gone. But physical attributes aside, my heart was still very much tied to his. I experienced strong emotions when he looked at me, or touched me... just minus the fireworks produced by the bond.

"I'm so sorry, Emma."

"Kade, don't. I'm sorry you were put in a position to make such a decision. You risked your life for me. You gave up your immortality, for *me*. I should be the one apologizing. Ever since I came into your life, I've brought nothing but pain."

"Emma, you have given my life hope and meaning. Up until the time I met you, I was living each day, just doing my job. The moment we touched, I had purpose. I now have a future to look forward to, if you so choose."

"How can I be so lucky?" I asked.

"*You* are lucky? No one even knows the dormant potential lying within you, which scares them. You could possibly be the key to ending the immortal war... and I am bonded to you." He slid down to his knees and nestled between my legs. "I happen to think that makes *me* the lucky one."

His words made me blush. "You're crazy. And adorable. But I sure don't feel like I have something hidden in me. If anything, I feel like I've lost my identity."

"No. You're finding your true identity. And some may have even seen glimpses of it in the Underworld."

"How would you know?" I asked.

"Because they told me," he grinned. "Do you realize it's nearly impossible to slay a Hellhound? Lucifer placed them at the last gate because immortals don't usually try and go up against them. But you, a mortal girl, comes strolling along and not only attempt an attack, but successfully slaughter them. That's pretty damn amazing, and just the tip of the iceberg." He squeezed my hands. "You're a dark horse, Emma. No one really knows your full potential, but I expect it will be mind-blowing. And, I'm glad I was chosen to be a part of your journey."

I pulled his hands around my waist and left them there, resting my arms on his shoulders. "We're lucky to have each other."

"Everything will work out in the end. We just have to believe," he said softly.

"I really hope so. I just wish there was some way for you to become immortal again."

"Hey. Don't you worry about me. I may not be as strong as I used to be, but I can still kick some serious ass. And, I will always be here to protect you."

"Thank you. I know you will. I will never doubt that," I said. "But are you sure there is no way for them to change you back?"

He shook his head. "I realize my decision is not one most immortals would make, but I'm totally fine with it. Besides, I've always wondered what it would be like to grow old. Now I'll get to experience it firsthand."

"And, what about me?"

"Once your transformation is complete, you're aging process will slow. It never stops, it just decelerates. Lucifer and Lucian have been around centuries longer than the rest of us, which is why they look a little more... distinguished."

"So, are there different kinds of Angels?"

"No, but we're given different titles as we progress. Every level completed brings you closer to the top. Being a Guardian is the first level, so you will notice most of them appear younger...and in Dom's case...immature. Guardians also take on a lot of human traits because they spend most of their time amongst them, intending to blend in."

"Well, that explains a lot," I laughed. Even though our Guardians were centuries old, they acted just like the boys in high school. But I was glad for that. Having them around kept things light and made life bearable. That, and the fact they were all drop-dead gorgeous.

The conversation came to a lull and I could see Kade had his own burning questions.

"I know you're probably wondering about Ethon," I whispered.

His eyes lowered. "Yeah. What did he mean when he said you were bonded?"

"Well, I don't know how or why, but when he introduced himself and our hands touched, I bonded with him. The same way I had with you," I breathed, butterflies turning madly in my stomach.

Should I tell him about the dreams? He hadn't ever lied to me, so I should show him the same courtesy.

"I don't understand," he said, wanting specifics.

"After you came back, changed, I started having these strange dreams. You were in them, but there were also these bright red eyes. When I first met him, I realized they belonged to Ethon. Each dream offered me the same choice. I didn't understand it at the time, but as I'm telling you now, I can see it. I think what Alaine said might be correct. Within me is both good and evil, dark and light. I have been bonded to both sides, and now I have to make a decision. What side do I want to be on?"

Kade squeezed his arms around me and pulled me to the edge of the bed. "You don't need to make any decisions soon. I realize there isn't anything serious between us right now, but I hope there will be."

I slid off the bed and landed on my knees in front of him, bodies pressed tight with the bed at my back. He held me, despite the stench of Hell lingering all over. He never even flinched.

"Hey," he whispered.

There was an undeniable attraction, pulling us together.

Before I could take another breath, his irresistible mouth took possession of mine. Using the bed as leverage, he trapped me, tight against his body.

The kiss was magical. It was so raw and intense. I parted my lips and our kiss deepened; tongues dancing in perfect unison. Afraid to touch his back, for fear it wasn't healed yet, I wrapped my arms tightly around his head to hold him in place.

He suddenly stood up, pulling me with him. The movement was so sudden, I gasped and wrapped my legs around his waist.

Shuffling a few steps, Kade placed me on a desk. I put my hands out to support our weight and he began a trail of hot kisses down my neck. My body quivered, and a moan of pleasure escaped my lips. He was pure magic, and I was completely under his spell.

His lips found mine again, our kiss deepening, filled with even stronger passion. I couldn't begin to imagine the emotion behind the sealing of a bond. The consummation of two, becoming one for all eternity.

Our lips parted suddenly, and he rested his forehead on mine. Both of us were panting heavily.

"God, I missed you, Emma," he said between breaths.

"I can tell," I whispered. I saw a grin sneak up on the corners of his mouth. "I missed you too."

"You have no idea," he stressed. "Leaving you - not knowing if you were hurt - nearly crushed me. I hated not being able to be there with you. It was the only time I despised my decision of becoming mortal. I prayed, every single day that you would come back to me, so I could hold you again."

"I know exactly how you were feeling. My heart nearly broke watching you in so much pain. The thought of losing you absolutely terrified me, I came so close to giving up."

"I'm glad you didn't. I knew you would make it. But I still can't believe you're here. It's as if you're back from the dead. Four months was a very, very long wait," he said, with a pained look.

"I'm here now," I said. A sudden wave of tiredness made me yawn.

"You must be exhausted," he observed.

"I am. And I need a really hot shower."

"Yeah. I'm pretty sure you'll feel a lot better after taking one," he chuckled and scrunched his nose.

"I stink, don't I?"

His lips tightened. "Well, I totally blame that on the Devil and his son. Their stink is nearly impossible to get rid of," he scoffed.

I laughed. "Then I better prepare for lots of bubbles and an extra-long soak."

Kade stood up and pulled me off the desk.

"I wish I could help you with that," he teased, "But, there are too many eyes watching out for you now." A devious smile rose on his face. "Besides, there is only so much restraint this new mortal body can endure, and I don't want to push it."

"Believe me...I know," I giggled. Tippy-toeing to give him one last kiss, I said, "I'll see you later." Then headed for the door.

"See you later."

As I stepped into the hall, Dominic, Malachi, Thomas, and Alexander were sitting on the stairs talking amongst themselves. I dreaded the thought of walking past them because I knew they would have something negative to say. I had one more flight of stairs to get up to my room, and no way of avoiding them. I was probably the topic of their heated discussion, and at this moment, invisibility was what I needed. I wondered if the suit could still make me invisible.

I wished and wished, but it didn't work. *Dammit.*

Dominic's voice called out. "Hey, Emma. Are you alright?" He must have thought I was going to pass out, standing there with my eyes tightly shut, wishing to disappear.

"Hey Dom," I smiled, "I'm fine." I quickly made my way to the stairway.

"You look like you're in a hurry," he said.

"I am. I'd like to wash Hell off me as quickly as possible. It's giving me a headache," I said, trying to avoid eye contact with any of them. I could feel their stares, wondering, waiting for me to give them some kind of answer to what happened earlier.

"Yeah, I'd like to wash away the stench you dragged in too," Malachi blurted.

I knew it would never go away, but all I could think about right now, was a hot shower, and falling into a deep, restful sleep with no dreams.

"Sorry, boys. If you're looking for answers, I don't have any for you right now," I said, stepping past them and bounding up the stairs.

"I'm sure we'll find out soon enough," Malachi answered. Their voices went low again, murmuring amongst themselves.

TWO

I QUICKLY MADE MY WAY down the hall to my bedroom. As soon as I was inside, I snapped the door shut behind me and locked it.

Finally. I was alone.

Standing here for a moment, the complete silence became a bit unnerving. Ever since I left to find Caleb in the caves, I hadn't been alone. Mixed emotions swirled through me. On one hand, I was happy because I could finally breathe and was safe - for the moment. On the other hand, I was alone…

The curtains were drawn, making the room dark and eerie. Clicking on the light, the first thing I noticed was my spotless room. Someone had cleaned while I was away. Quickly, I made my way to the dresser, pulled out pajamas, and headed for the bathroom.

As soon as I stepped inside and clicked on the light, I gasped, taken aback by the figure staring back at me. She looked tired and weary, blood and dirt smeared all over. Her face was war-torn, and strands of misplaced hair hung over her brown eyes. She had changed so much from the last time I saw her.

Slowly peeling off my super suit, I dropped it in the hamper. As soon as I became disconnected from it, overwhelming feelings of sadness and loss rushed over me. Its magic must have been holding me together. The emotions were so unbearable, I quickly turned on the bathwater to drown out the sounds of my uncontrollable sobs.

As soon as the bath was filled, I sunk deep into the hot bubbles, trying not to let the sadness drown me. Here, I could release my emotions and not worry about anyone seeing or hearing me, and it felt good.

I had been strong and tried to hold myself together to finish our quest. And I did survive, doing whatever I had to. I pulled every ounce of strength and courage out from depths I never knew existed, and now, all that remained were the remnants. Kade, Samuel, and Alaine were the silver lining in my new dark world.

I stayed in the tub until the water turned cold, and then dragged myself out and dressed for bed. Before my pruny-butt turned in for the night, I decided to boot up my laptop and check my email. Lia and Jeremy must have been going crazy wondering what happened to me for the past four months. Lia was such a worry wart, and I had a feeling my email was probably filled with her concerned messages. Knowing Lia, she probably thought I'd been mauled by a bear.

"OMG," I breathed out loud. Sure enough there were 47 new email messages, mainly from Lia, and a few from Jeremy. Most of the subject lines read: *HELLO?* Or, *Are you alive?* Or, *WTH?*

I clicked on the most recent email which was written two days ago from Lia.

Emma,

What the hell? I just called again, and your Aunt said you were camping and didn't have service wherever you were. Damn it, girl!!! Is there service anywhere in that damn state? I've been trying to contact you for the past four months, and haven't heard a single word back. You better have a good excuse. I swear I sprouted another white hair today, all thanks to you.

Any-how...school sucks without you. But, OMG! I can't wait to come and visit you. Total hug fest! Jeremy and I will be there in four days! Eeeeeek! I swear, Emma, you'd better be back from camping by then, and you better message me. If you're dead, I will resurrect you and slap you silly for giving me grief, white hair, and making me constantly worry about you. Well, you can spill when we get there.

So, is Kade still in the picture? Did he go camping with you? OMG. I still have visions of his yummy self in my head. You are so dang lucky. I will see you very soon!

Oh! Our visit is supposed to be a surprise, so don't say anything and act surprised! Lol

Hugs and kisses,

Lia

Okay, wait... *What?*

I had to pause and re-read the part about her coming in four days. I quickly scrolled down and clicked on previous emails. I gasped, my head started spinning a million miles an hour.

It was true. But they weren't coming in four days, they were coming in two!

Holy crap!

My heart instantly dropped and was filled with a sense of impending doom. They couldn't come here. Not right now. This place wasn't safe. I had to talk to Alaine in the morning. She must have given them the okay to come, but why?

As much as I wanted to see Jeremy and Lia again, I knew there was a real danger outside. But they already made their plans, and seriously, there was no way to tell them no. Lia wouldn't dare pass up a trip to get away from her parents and visit me.

What was I supposed to tell them? That they couldn't come because we were in the middle of an immortal war, and I was being hunted by a mad, murderous Fallen Angel who wanted to either kill, or capture me for his wicked gain? That'd go over like a fart in a spacesuit.

And how the heck was I supposed to explain about the Guardians or *Lucifer's son*?

All I could do was wait until morning and see what Alaine had to say about it. Until then, I would have to respond to Lia's email. The key was brevity.

Hey Lia,

First…Holy crap! Are you seriously coming??? Oh my God. I almost dropped from a heart attack when I read your message. My heart is still pounding and I'm hyperventilating.

Second...I'm ALIVE! I promise. I still don't have a cell phone, but there is no need for resurrection.

I'm so sorry I didn't get back to you sooner, but the service here is horrible, and they've taken me all over this godforsaken state on an adventure to try and take my mind off of everything. Believe me, there isn't much to see, unless you love landscapes of endless trees. It is beautiful though.

Yes, Kade is still here, and I've spent quite a bit of time with him. I'll spill when you get here. Nothing major, but I really like him, and I know he likes me too.

Well, I better get to bed. We just got back from camping and I'm wiped. Don't worry, I will totally act surprised. I can't wait to see and hug you both. It feels like it's been forever.

Love you,
Emma

That message should tide her over until she arrived, and I knew she'd let Jeremy know I was okay. I suddenly yawned, and felt the lack of sleep catch up to me. My eyelids felt like lead weights had been attached to them, and my limbs were so weak they were shaking.

I shut down the laptop and jumped into bed, pulling the warm blankets over me. I relaxed and sunk my head into the soft pillow. I seriously took for granted the things which seemed so insignificant. Things like how amazingly wonderful sleeping on a real bed felt. I'd slept on rocks, in Hell, for the past week. Now, I felt like I was lying on a cloud. Snuggling in deeper, I pulled the covers up over my neck, and closed my eyes. In a matter of seconds, sleep found me.

I woke and was greeted with darkness, but the light outside was trying to peek in through the cracks. I debated whether or not to get out of bed, but my stomach insisted on it. It was demanding to be fed.

A quick glance at the clock told me it was 12:12pm. Sheeze, I'd slept the whole morning away.

Begrudgingly, I peeled myself from the warmth of the blankets and shivered as I headed over to pull back the curtains. The sky was dark and gray. Heavy clouds hung in the sky making the world look even drearier.

My insides twisted at the sight of the labyrinth. What was supposed to be a beautiful work of art, brought back a rush of negative emotions.

The cottage looked cozy and had a column of smoke rising from its chimney.

I inhaled the cool air, then headed to the closet and grabbed a pair of blue jeans, a black t-shirt and, a dark gray hoodie to coordinate with the day.

Inside the bathroom I caught my reflection again. It was amazing what a night's rest could do. My hair was a matted mess, but at least I didn't look like the walking dead. I quickly brushed my teeth, my hair, and applied some foundation, eyeliner, and lip-gloss. Lastly, I placed the Bloodstone amulet back around my neck. It had become my personal, warning-of-danger accessory.

After a quick assessment and agreeing I looked like a normal human being, I headed out the door. As soon as I stepped out of my room, I saw a figure charging at me from down the hall.

"Morning, Emma!" Courtney sang. She was carrying a muffin in her hand. Blueberry. I heard my stomach rumble again.

"Morning, Courtney," I smiled.

"You slept in late. I was waiting for you to get up," she noted.

"You were? Were you waiting in the hall for me?"

"No, silly. I just came up from the kitchen. Miss Lily has lunch ready if you're hungry, and there are still some yummy blueberry muffins left from breakfast."

My mouth began to water as I eyed her yummy goods. "That looks really good."

"It is, but lunch is way better. She made fried chicken, corn, and mashed potatoes with gravy. You better hurry because all the boys are down there. I even saw those two scary, huge guys in the kitchen."

"Alright, I'm on it," I said. "Thanks for the info."

"No problem. Oh! And Alaine wanted me to tell you that she wants to see you in her study. She's there now, so you'd better go there first."

"Okay, thanks. I'll see you later," I smiled.

"Maybe we can watch a movie or play a board game?" She asked with a raised brow.

"I'd like that," I replied.

Her face lit up, happy with my answer. "Alright, I'll come find you later," she said. Turning around, she skipped to her room and disappeared inside.

I smiled as I made my way toward the stairway, and was

surprised at how quiet it was. Everyone must have been having lunch. The thought of food sent my stomach complaining again. The whole area was empty, so I bounced down the stairs and then made a right down the hall to Alaine's study.

When I arrived at her door, I knocked and immediately heard her answer.

"Come in."

I twisted the knob and entered. The sweet smell of roses greeted me.

"You wanted to see me?" I asked.

"Yes. Please come in and have a seat," she said. She was seated behind her computer, but as soon as she saw me, her chocolate brown eyes sparkled. Her face was luminous and looked like porcelain; her dark, silky hair cascaded down in large ringlets. She was beautiful, and I did see a lot of me in her.

I headed toward her desk and took a seat facing her. She reached across and brushed my cheek with her hand.

"Good afternoon, sweetheart. How was your sleep?"

"It was great. I actually knocked out and don't think I moved once," I giggled.

"That's great. You needed to rest and heal," she said. "I wanted to discuss a few things with you, but first, I wanted to tell you how very proud I am. You really held your own in the Underworld. The boys keep saying how amazed they were at your strength. You saved them, and I cannot thank you enough for taking care of them and Samuel."

"I really didn't do much. Dominic and Malachi arrived just in time save Samuel, and Danyel...well, he was the one who saved me. If he didn't come when he did, I would have ended up being a Grimlock snack."

I tried to make light of it, but Danyel's face suddenly flashed before my eyes. I could vividly see his eyes, and hear the last words he spoke to me before the Hellhound ripped out his throat. I instantly curled up and felt sick.

Before a tear could escape my eyes, Alaine was there, wrapping her arms around me.

"It's alright, sweetheart. You've had so much pain and sadness. It's okay to cry."

I did cry. I cried and cried, until I couldn't cry anymore - and she never let go. She stroked my hair and hugged me. I cried for my parents, and for Danyel, and for the pain that Samuel and Kade had to endure. The sadness had been bottled up for so long, every time it was shaken... it exploded.

I'd hoped to keep it inside, and deal with it myself, but I couldn't. It overflowed from me, and there was no way of stopping it.

After it was over, I felt a release. I felt like I could move on and start over. My heart would forever have a piece missing, but I knew if I gave up, the people who lost their lives for me would be heartbroken. I would have to move on and make them proud. I would live my life so they did not die in vain. I knew my parents and Danyel would look down on me and smile.

"I'm sorry," I said, wiping my face dry.

"Emma," Alaine said softly. "Don't be sorry. Sometimes it's

good to grieve. It helps the healing process."

I nodded.

"One of the things I wanted to share with you is that I set up funeral arrangements for your parents. They will be buried on-site, right outside of the property. We have a small cemetery, where Courtney and Caleb's mother, and my late husband are buried. It's a small plot, but it's a beautiful place to be laid to rest.

I think once the funeral is complete you will have some kind of closure. All of their belongings are being packed and will be shipped here. I will put them in storage until you decide what you want to do with it."

"Thank you so much," I said. I was glad I would have a final chance to say goodbye to my parents. They deserved to rest in a beautiful place.

"Of course. I loved my sister. I also wanted to set something up to have Danyel's ashes spread."

"That's great," I breathed.

"There is one more thing I wanted to talk to you about," she said, her brow furrowed.

"Is it about my friends coming to visit?"

Her eyes widened. "Yes. That's exactly what I wanted to talk to you about."

"Yeah, Lia can't keep secrets."

"Well, they called me the day you left LA, and asked if they could come and visit you during their break. I told them it was fine, because at the time, there was no immediate threat. I think we can manage four days. This will be good for you. You need to try and relax and have some fun. I also thought it would be a good idea for them to attend the funeral, since they were close to Victoria and Christian. Unless you don't think that's a good idea."

The sound of my parents' names made my heart ache horribly. I swallowed the huge lump in my throat, and fought the urge to weep again.

"No, that's a great idea. My parents loved them, and vice versa. I know they would want to attend, and it will be great to have them there for support."

"Then I'll finish the arrangements. We can spread Danyel's ashes after they leave, since they don't know him. It's a place Samuel chose, so we might have to fly, which means Ethon and his friends will have to join us."

"Okay," I agreed.

Then, as if she could read my mind, she added, "I know you're confused about the whole double bonding, and I am just as baffled. But just because it has chosen, doesn't mean you have to make a decision right now."

"You and Kade have an incredibly strong connection. The first time I saw the two of you together, it reminded me of when I met Samuel. I know why the bond would choose Kade. He is an honorable young man, and I know he would take great care of you. As for the bond with Ethon, well that is something I am still unsure of. But we cannot deny that it chose him."

"All I can suggest is that you take it slow. Get to know each one of them fully before you make your final decision…because once the bond is sealed, it is forever. Don't rush it, and don't feel like you have to shun Ethon."

"As much as I'd like to dislike him, he was placed in our lives for a reason. He never chose the bond, the bond chose him."

Alaine paused and then added one more piece of advice. "Keep your heart guarded, but also open enough to feel what the truth is. I believe in you, Emma, and know when the time comes… you will make the right decision."

"Thank you," I said, hugging her.

"And always remember that Samuel and I will be here for you. We have loved you from the moment you took your first breath."

"Thank you, for everything," I breathed, fighting the urge to cry. "I'm sorry things turned out the way they did, and I understand you only wanted the best for me. I appreciate you and Samuel for that, and I love you too."

"You don't know how much that means to me," she smiled, and wiped her tear.

We both stood with tears in our eyes, and then suddenly started laughing.

"Have you eaten anything?" Alaine asked.

"Not yet, but I heard Miss Lily made fried chicken for lunch."

"She did, and you better head over there quickly because all the boys are there now."

"I will," I laughed.

"Remember, Emma. Don't let anyone push you into sealing the bond. It's hard to resist, and sometimes if you put yourself into a position…well…" She blushed. I could tell she was embarrassed, and having a hard time trying to convey the message to *be safe*. She was just being a mom. If my mom was here, she would have just come right out and said...*Don't you dare have sex with any of these boys, Emma. Not until you make it right first!*

"Don't worry. There won't be any bond sealing anytime soon," I reassured her.

She exhaled loudly and placed her hand to her heart. "Thank God. I'm glad we got that out of the way."

"Yes," I giggled. "I'll see you later."

"Bye sweetheart. And remember, you can be nice to Ethon," she smiled.

I nodded and headed out the door.

THREE

I FOLLOWED THE WONDERFUL AROMA wafting down the hallway, and as I rounded the corner to the kitchen, I was hit with an overwhelming dizziness and euphoric feeling.

Damn it.

Ethon was close.

I was about to turn around when Alaine's words resounded loudly in my head.

I sighed. I guess I should be nice. She was right, it wasn't his fault the bond had chosen him. And, because of him, we did get out of hell free. Well, almost free. Someone would have to pay a price for our freedom, but I didn't want to think about that right now.

As soon as I stepped into the kitchen, I was hit with the smell of heaven, and was immediately greeted by Miss Lily.

"Emma! Oh dear Lord, it's so good to see you again." Her face lit up when she saw me.

"Hi, Miss Lily. It's great to see you again, and so good to be back," I answered.

From the corner of my eye, I saw a figure shift. I turned and, lo and behold, it was Ethon.

As soon as our eyes connected there was an electric buzz filling the air. I saw him glance down, avoiding eye contact, probably trying to fight the immense pull of the bond.

"Hey Emma," he said, quickly glancing back up to me.

"Hey, Ethon. So how's the tower?" As soon as the words left my mouth I felt completely lame. I hope he didn't feel like was banished or something. Well, Alaine did banish them, but for good reason. I couldn't have both of the boys I was bonded with in the same house. They'd rip each other to shreds.

"The tower is fine. Alaine has been a gracious host and has provided us with whatever we need," he answered. I had a feeling he wanted to say more, but didn't.

His eyes captured mine again, and as they did, I couldn't help but feel a deep seeded connection. Damn this bond. It was just as strong with Ethon as it had been with Kade. I hated that it was putting me in this position.

Ethon's crimson eyes were even darker now, and I awed at the perfect and strong definitions of his facial features. Unknowingly, my eyes slowly wandered down, and I began taking in his well-defined arms and chest, and finally resting on his ridiculous abs.

My mind started to wonder why the bond had chosen him. What was it about him that connected us?

The room began to feel heated. I swallowed the lump growing in my throat, and as I glanced back up, a grin graced his lips.

Oh. My. God. He just noticed me, noticing him. That was slightly mortifying.

Instantly blushing, I turned away. My emotions and insides were going haywire. I closed my eyes to pull myself back together.

"Here you go, Ethon. I hope you enjoy it," Miss Lily said. I opened my eyes as she was handing him a plate of food. Two pieces of crispy fried chicken, corn, and mashed potatoes smothered in gravy.

"Beautiful," he said, but was staring straight at me. "Thank you, Miss Lily. I greatly appreciate it, and am sure I will enjoy every bite." He smiled at her, and it made my insides melt.

"Well, I better go," he said. "I'll see you around, Emma."

"Yes, I'm sure I'll be running into you soon. Have your friends eaten?" I asked. I really didn't care about them, but I thought it was a nice gesture. As much as I wanted not to like Ethon, the power of the bond wouldn't allow me to. It filled my heart with compassion, and desire, which kept me from pushing him away.

"Yes, they have eaten and they've also come back for seconds." Ethon rolled his eyes and shook his head. "I'm sorry Miss Lily. They couldn't resist your sinfully delicious food."

"Oh, don't you worry about that. It just means I'm doing my job, and doing it well." She laughed, and her laughter became contagious.

"Well, ladies, I wish you both a good day," Ethon said with a crooked grin. He then turned and headed out the door.

I held my breath and waited for the dizziness to subside, and in a few moments, the pull of the bond released and I started to feel normal again.

Holy crap on a cracker.

Miss Lily started working on making me a plate. With her eyes still on her work, I heard. "It seems you have a few boys on your tail." She quickly glanced up and smiled.

My eyes widened. "You have no idea, Miss Lily."

"Oh, I think I have a pretty good idea. I may only be the cook here, but I work in the central area of this house. I see and hear almost everything going on. I know the truth about the residents in this house, and haven't been told anything directly."

"I know they aren't of this world, but I also know they are good and wouldn't bring harm to anyone who didn't deserve it. I just keep my mouth shut and do my job. I'm not paid to get into anyone's business, and I don't go looking for it."

Miss Lily's eyes suddenly fixed on mine. "I overheard them talking about the Immortal Bond. Now, I know it's not my place to speak, but I thought that I'd give you a little feedback. I have a gift of seeing people's auras."

"Oh, I'd love your feedback." I leaned in closer to her.

"I've come into contact with both boys and both of them have good, healthy auras. I've known Kade for a while now. He is a good person, and would be a great choice. He would give his life for you. On the other hand, I also have a feeling Ethon would do the same. I know where he comes from, but the aura around him is not evil. There are some dark edges, but we all have those."

"What I'm trying to say is don't close your heart. Don't make a decision based on what you see. Make the decision based on what your heart tells you. You have a very good heart, Emma, and a very strong, bright aura. When the time comes, I know you will choose correctly. Either boy will make a fine catch. Hell, if I were younger, I'd take one off your hands," she rolled with laughter.

"I wish you could. They would be lucky to have you," I said, winking at her. "If I was a guy, I'd swipe you up in a second. You have the key to a man's heart – through his stomach."

"Oh, my dear child. You are too kind. I don't envy you one bit. You are like a caterpillar in a cocoon, waiting for your time. Every trial and every tribulation is molding your destiny. One day, you will emerge as a beautiful butterfly."

"Thank you, Miss Lily," I said. "I do feel like I'm in a cocoon right now, but am terrified I will never be released."

"Oh, you will, dear. You will." Miss Lily, handed me a hot plate of food. "Just believe in yourself."

I took in a deep breath of the hot food. "Oh my goodness. I haven't had a hot meal in…well, since the last time I was here."

"Oh dear child, you better get your skinny butt in there and eat! No one will starve on my watch."

"You don't have to tell me twice," I said. "Thanks so much for the advice."

"Anytime, child. Anytime," she said, shooing me toward the dining room.

FOUR

S I WALKED TOWARD THE dining area, I could hear boisterous voices. I wondered what I would be walking into, and if I really wanted to put myself in the middle of a debate. Whatever. Right now, they knew just as much as I did.

I sucked in a deep breath and proceeded with my plate. As soon as I entered the room they all stood and started clapping and whooping.

"There's our slayer," Dominic cheered, waving his fork in the air.

"Emma, I heard you kicked some Hellhound ass," Alexander added. "Damn, I wish I was there to see it."

"She freaking saved my life, and I'm not ashamed to say it. I have a whole limb because of her," Dominic announced.

I blushed and didn't know what to say. I hated being the center of attention and it felt completely odd. I liked being invisible.

I noticed Kade's beautiful, beaming face at the end of the table, and decided to head toward him. I quickly walked past the guys, blushing. They held out their hands and I smacked them with high-fives.

"Emma, you have to teach me some of your moves," Thomas said, his eyebrows wiggled.

"Can you all just leave her alone," James butted in. "Just let her eat in peace."

I liked James, and never really had the chance to get to know him. He was the oldest of the bunch and Alaine's Guardian. From what I knew, he seemed to be knowledgeable and very helpful. He was close with Alaine, so he must be a pretty awesome guy.

"Thank you," I mouthed as I passed him by.

He tipped his head and smiled. "They're just excited. They haven't had this much excitement in over a century, especially from a girl who can fight as well as any of them."

I shook my head. "It wasn't me. It was the suit and the dagger. Their magic did something to me and made me do things I never thought I could do."

James looked at me with a certain glint in his eye. "There is a lot you need to learn about immortal objects. They are magical, yes, but their magic feeds off of the user. It might have aided you, but that's it. What you did came from inside of you."

I didn't know what to say. I was dumbfounded.

"Thank you," I said.

Kade pulled out the seat next to him.

"Thanks."

"My pleasure," he grinned. "So how was your sleep?"

"Too good. I almost slept the whole day away."

"You should have. Sleep helps the healing process. You look ninety-nine percent better than yesterday."

"Tell me about it. I don't know how you could look at me, let alone touch me last night."

There was silence and a loud clearing of a throat. Looking over, I saw the familiar glare from Malachi across the table.

"It wasn't like that," Kade assured him.

"Yeah? It better not be. You two need to be supervised. The last thing I need is for my boy's new mortal ass to be buried out back by Alaine or Samuel," he grumbled.

Dominic yelled from the other side of the table, "Hey Emma. You can tell those smelly ass demons to crawl back to the pit from whence they came." They all started laughing.

"Yeah, we can handle Lucian on our own. We don't need them," Alexander added.

"And screw that freaking bond," Dominic sneered. "Our boy Kade is a million times the Angel that Devil-boy will ever be."

"*Used* to be," Kade corrected. I could tell by the tone of his voice, he was a bit miffed. I could totally understand him feeling inferior to Ethon, but I wasn't going to make my decision based on that.

"Well, they better keep their distance, and stay in that damn tower. The last thing we need is the enemy inside, watching, and learning everything about us. They could be working with Lucian for all we know. This could all be a set up. Our defenses are already down with them inside," Dominic huffed.

"It just means we need to stay on high alert, and make sure Emma and Alaine stay safe," James added. "They are our main priority."

"That means no going outside unattended," Malachi said, shooting a glance at me.

"I don't have a death wish," I answered.

"Good. If you absolutely have to go outside, you'd better make sure we know about it, and you have someone with you," he added.

"Emma's friends will be visiting in a few days, so you will all have to be even more watchful," James noted.

He didn't sound too happy about it, and I didn't expect him to. I knew having Lia and Jeremy here would really complicate things. They already had enough stress watching Alaine and I. Adding Jeremy and Lia to the mix was an added strain. But I knew my friends. They would be happy staying indoors watching movies and eating popcorn.

"You have two friends coming?" Dominic asked with a raised brow.

"I do, but one is a dude," I chuckled. "And they are off limits. I don't want them involved in anything remotely dangerous."

"Emma, are you kidding? They are coming to the worst possible place for danger," Dominic said, shaking his head.

"Well, they need to feel like there is no danger at all. That will be our mission this week," James stepped in again. I was really beginning to like him. He was a true leader. "Alaine will brief you all soon."

"Don't worry, Emma. They will be safe. Four days will come and go very quickly. You never know when you'll get another chance to be with them, so make it count," Kade said.

"Thank you," I breathed.

"Alright guys, let her eat," Kade scolded.

"Fine," Dominic jested. "I'll bug the slayer later." He smiled, and then pushed back his chair and exited the room.

"It was nice to finally properly meet you," James said, getting up from the table. He came over and held out his hand, and I shook it. "I hope we will get a chance to talk more."

"I'm sure we will, and thanks for sticking up for me," I said.

"A pleasure." He smiled and followed the rest of the guys out.

"See you guys around," Thomas called out.

"Yeah, see you later," Alexander repeated.

"Bye," I said as they walked out.

Malachi was the only one left, finishing the last scoop of corn.

His chair squeaked as he pushed it backwards. "I'll be keeping an eye on you two." He then turned with his plate and walked out.

"Love you too, Malachi," I teased. I heard him growl and it made me laugh.

Kade and I were left alone. "Okay, eat," he said.

I picked up the piece of chicken and bit into it. It was crunchy, but the inside was moist and juicy. I moaned as the flavor hit my mouth.

"Good huh?"

"Oh my goodness."

I then scooped up some mashed potatoes. It was like a glorious cloud of buttery goodness which melted in my mouth. The corn was so sweet, and in no time my plate was clean. I didn't even realize how fast I'd eaten.

"Do you want more?" Kade chuckled, breaking the silence.

"No, thank you. I'm full, and that was embarrassing," I giggled. "I knew I was hungry, but didn't think I'd eat like a T-rex."

"Are you sure?" he asked.

"Yes," I said, wiping my mouth.

He took my plate and placed it on his, then stood and pulled my chair out.

"Always a gentleman," I chimed.

"I try," he replied. As we made our way into the kitchen he asked, "Do you want to take a walk with me? I have something I want to show you."

"Outside?"

"Yes."

"Sure," I answered. "Aren't we supposed to let someone know?"

"You'll be with me, and believe me...they'll know. There are eyes all around this house, and they see everything. Well, mostly everything."

Kade walked over to the sink, rinsed the dishes, and loaded them into the dishwasher.

"You don't have to do that, sweet boy," Miss Lily said.

"I know, but you shouldn't have to either."

"Oh honey. It's part of my job. Besides, it keeps me busy, and I enjoy it. I truly do."

"Miss Lily, that was the tastiest meal I've ever had."

"Thank you, dear. You just made my day. I'll see you at dinner," she winked.

As we made our way out, Kade extended his arm, and I locked mine around his.

It didn't matter if the overwhelming pull of the bond was present. Whenever I was close to him, my insides twisted and my pulse raced. I felt happy.

There was just something about him from the first time we met. But now I *know* there is more than the bond connecting us. For one whole year he watched over me, making sure I was safe. That alone made my heart grow fonder.

He led me outside, and I was surprised at how warm it was, despite the darkness. It was, in my mind, only a few weeks ago that it was the dead of winter. Now we were headed into spring. The thaw started early, and the grass was already starting to show some color. Even the trees were filled with buds waiting to burst into bloom.

The air was colder today, because the sun was hidden behind a dark veil of clouds.

"Which way would you like to walk?" he asked.

"I have options?"

"You do. Left or right?"

"Let's go right." I didn't want to go left and pass the tower. I had a feeling Ethon and his goons would be watching. The thought sent a shiver down my spine.

I tightened my grip on Kade's arm, and he smiled.

"So what did you do for four months while I was gone?" I questioned, trying to make small talk and fill the quiet.

"Oh, mostly worried about you. The rest was just trying to heal and recover."

My heart ached, knowing he must have endured the worse kind of pain imaginable. I knew what a burn on the finger felt like. It hurt like heck. But to have that excruciating pain all over your back times one thousand... it was unthinkable. "I'm so sorry you had to go through that," I whispered.

"I'm not going to lie. It was pretty miserable in the beginning. But I managed to get through it by picturing your face. I wondered what you were enduring in the Underworld. I focused on healing quickly so I could get back to you. You helped me get through the worst part of the pain."

I didn't know how to respond. My heart swelled to the point of bursting.

"Is it alright now?" I swallowed.

"It is. There are hideous scars, but—"

Before he could finish, I pulled his arm, stopping him. He turned to me and I buried myself in his chest. His arms wrapped around me.

"I'm sorry. It was because of me. You shouldn't have turned around. I had the suit and you would have been fine."

"No. I wasn't going to take a chance with something I wasn't one hundred percent positive about, especially when it came to your safety."

I sobbed and he held me.

"Hey, no crying," he said.

I felt like a sap. I didn't want to cry, but it seemed like I was doing a lot of it lately. My emotions were going haywire. It didn't help that I was surrounded with darkness. But I needed to suck it up and be strong. I just hated the fact he had been in so much pain, and I wasn't there.

I quickly pulled myself together and wiped my tears. "So where are you taking me?"

"I'll show you," he said, taking my hand, and leading me around the house. As we rounded the corner, I had a crazy feeling of déjà vu. Towering in front of us was the labyrinth, covered in shredded plastic.

Anxiety flooded over me. A sense of doom hung in the air. Those creepy clouds were not helping the matter.

The labyrinth represented terror. It was *the* place which started the last series of ill-fated events: Caleb being kidnapped, the war with the Darkling, meeting Lucian, Kade becoming mortal, traveling into the Underworld, and all the pain and death which came with the journey... including my bond with Ethon.

"Has the secret entry been sealed?"

"Yes. Alaine had it filled in completely. There is no way to get in or out. The barrier covers the house and the labyrinth. The only things not covered are the cottage and tower, so we won't have to worry about the Fallen."

"I'm fine. Let's go," I said, stepping forward. He wanted me to go in with him for a reason, and I wasn't going to be the downer.

Wrapping his arm around my shoulder, he led us through the entrance – in the opposite direction Courtney had taken me the first time.

"Where are we going?"

"To the center."

"What's at the center?" Intrigue began to outweigh my anxiety.

"You'll see. It's the only place we can be alone, without any eyes." His eyes beamed, which made me smile.

We quickly made our way through the maze of foliage, weaving every-which-way, until we came to an area which had a canopy of foliage above us.

Kade led me through to the middle of the space, and I realized we had made it to the center. There were four walls of hedges surrounding us, but the edges were left open. He reached his hand inside one of them, pulling out a medium sized box, and then handed it to me.

"What's this?" I asked.

"Open it and see," he grinned.

I slowly peeled the lid back and gasped. Emotions overwhelmed me once again. The box contained hundreds of pictures of me and my parents. It was filled with the wonderful memories of my childhood.

"Kade, how did you—"

"As soon as I was well enough, I flew to LA and retrieved these before the movers came, and..." he held up a finger while reaching back into the hedge. "I also brought you this."

He handed me another box, and I immediately recognized it.

I grasped my mother's jewelry box. Opening it up, memories of her wearing these priceless treasures overwhelmed me. Hot tears trickled down my cheeks. Her earrings, necklaces, and rings were organized neatly in their spaces. I suddenly caught a familiar scent. Lifting the box to my nose, I breathed in deeply. Her perfume assaulted my senses. I grasped the box to my chest and hugged tightly, wishing it were my mom here instead.

"I don't know what to say. Thank you is not enough." I was supposed to be strong, but my heart was still broken.

Placing a comforting hand on my back, Kade replied, "You don't have to say anything. I just thought you'd like these, and hoped it might help you get through some tough times. I wanted to make your world a little brighter," he said softly.

His eyes were filled with so much love. "I cannot thank you enough," I exhaled, and curled into his warm embrace. His rare kindness never ceased to amaze me.

There was a sudden rush of wind around us, and as we glanced up Kade tightened his hold on me. Two large figures with black wings hovered above.

Bane and Azzah.

"How the hell did you get here? I thought the barrier was up?" Kade yelled up to them, using his body to shield me from them.

"There is no barrier here," Bane scoffed.

"Shit," Kade cursed. "What the hell is going on?"

"Take your hands off of the girl. She's Ethon's property."

"That's bullshit! She is property of no one, especially that bastard."

"Step away, mortal, or we'll tear your arms off," Bane growled.

I hated the way they referred to him as a mortal. They knew it was degrading, and were purposely baiting him.

"I'd like to see you try," Kade yelled back. There wasn't one ounce of fear in his eyes.

"Hey!" I yelled, stepping forward. I didn't want Kade to get hurt, and knew the goons would have no problem inflicting injury. I didn't want to take a chance. "Why don't you black birds just fly away? Kade is right. I'm *no one's* property, and I don't appreciate you hovering over us, interrupting our personal conversation." I was letting my emotions get the best of me.

A heat started to emanate on my chest, and when I glanced down, the Bloodstone amulet was glowing bright red. *What the— ?*

Suddenly Malachi, Dominic, and Thomas came rushing toward us with their weapons drawn.

"What the hell is going on?" Kade asked.

"Dude," Thomas urged. "I hate to break up your little moment, but there are dozens of Darkling headed this way. I suggest you get her out of here."

"I thought Darkling don't come out during the day?" I questioned.

"No sun, and we're in the boonies. They must have been close, waiting for the right time to strike," Malachi answered.

Loud growls filled the air; the overwhelming stench of Darkling surrounded us.

"Shit! It's too late," Dominic cursed. "They're inside the gates. Kade, keep Emma behind us. We'll protect you."

"I'll make sure she's safe. Just do what you gotta do," Kade answered.

"Bane! Azzah! What the hell are you waiting for? Go and kill some freaking Darkling!" Ethon scolded. He'd suddenly appeared out of nowhere, and was standing right behind us.

Bane and Azzah, still in flight, growled, and then drew their swords and flew off toward the gates. Loud screams of pain ensued.

41

More Darkling came bursting though the labyrinth. This was becoming a place I would *never* enter again. It was a never-ending nightmare.

Thomas yelled and charged forward with his sword overhead. A Darkling charged him, and he pushed his sword straight through its heart. "That's one!" he cheered.

"Who the hell's counting?" Malachi scolded. "Just kill the damn stinkers."

"I'm counting...starting now," Dominic said, unsheathing his two short-swords. He ran forward, flipped in the air, and pushed his first blade into the head of a Darkling just breaking through the brush. Without an interruption in movement, he spun around and took the head off a second one. Black blood, thick like tar, began spewing all over.

Another one charged him, but he spun like a whirlwind, sinking his blade straight in the Darkling's eye. Its anguished scream pierced our ears as it dropped to its knees. Dominic placed his foot to its skull, yanked his blade free, sliced off its head, and kicked it over.

"And that makes three," he said, aiming his words at Thomas.

"Whatever, Dude. There are lots more coming this way. And this time, you're scrubbing *my* sword. I even bought you a new set of gloves. Purple...with daisies."

Dominic rolled with laughter. "Oh, I think daisies suit you best. And the purple would complement your delicate complexion. Plus, you seem to have perfected the art of cleaning bloody blades, I think you should stick with it."

"Screw you, dude," Thomas huffed. "I'll be making mine extra crappy, just for you."

Ethon stepped closer to us and extended his hand out to me.

"Stay the hell away from her," Kade said, shielding me again.

"Emma, come with me. I can get you out of here, and take you to safety."

I paused, totally bewildered, feeling pulled in both directions

"I said, step away from her," Kade warned, grasping his sword.

"Kade, don't let him take her," Malachi roared.

"Are you a freaking idiot? I can outfly those bastards and take her to safety," Ethon rebuked.

Kade hesitated. His eyes swirled with uncertainty, warring within himself.

"Kade!" Malachi growled, but his eyes were still focused on the oncoming terror.

"Are you seriously thinking of risking her life, keeping her in the middle of danger?" Ethon's crimson eyes burned like fire. His face was hard-set and serious.

"I swear, if you lay one hand on her, I will find you...and I will kill you," Kade threatened.

Kade suddenly loosened his grip on me. At the same time Ethon stepped forward and wrapped his arm around my waist, tugging me against him, locking our bodies firmly together. I gasped as the power of the bond shot an electrical current through my body. I weakened and almost buckled, but Ethon tightened his grip. He glanced down at me with a crooked grin, and then shot a quick glare at Kade.

"Smart move, lover boy. I won't lay a hand on her, but I'm not making any promises to keep the other hand to myself." As soon as he finished speaking, we shot into the air.

"Kade," I screamed, terrified. The sound of the whipping wind muffled my cry.

"What the hell did you do?" Malachi rebuked.

Against my better judgment, I glanced down at the mass of Darkling bodies climbing over the gates, surrounding the labyrinth. We were outnumbered and had a full on battle on our hands. But I had faith in the Guardians. I knew they could kick ass, especially Darkling.

FIVE

W E WERE FLYING SO FAST, I was having a hard time catching my breath. Once we were high in the sky, I started to feel lightheaded.

A chilling shrill pierced the dark sky. It was Ash, circling above, alerting us of danger. In the distance, two Fallen angels were flying fast in our direction.

"Oh my God," I screamed.

"Your God can't help you now, but I can. And I suggest you hold on tight," Ethon ordered.

I didn't hesitate. Wrapping my legs around his waist, and tightening my arms around his neck, I locked them in. At the same time, his arms tightened around me, pulling me even closer against him. In a flash we took off, and everything around us became in a blur. Ethon was flying so fast, I swear we broke the sound barrier. I became dizzy so I had to close my eyes.

I felt his face press against mine. Tingles pricked my cheek as he spoke in my ear. "You okay?"

I nodded.

"I'll slow down in a minute. Those Fallen are probably wondering where the hell we went, but I don't want to take any chances. Not with you. I'm taking you to a secret place where you will be safe for the time being."

I nodded again. Not only was it difficult to talk with the wind whipping all around me – but even more distracting – Ethon's soft lips moving against my ear as he spoke. How was a girl supposed to form sentences under these circumstances?

"I thought you liked to fly?"

"I do, but not at deadly, supersonic speeds," I breathed.

Ethon laughed. "Don't worry. I can see fine. It's part of my gift. Perfect vision no matter what speed. I'll let you know when it's safe to open your eyes."

"Thanks," I said. His warm cheek was still pressed tightly against mine. His scent had a calming effect. It was so intoxicating, I found myself burrowing my face into the crook of his neck and breathing deeply. It was sweet and spicy, with a hit of smokiness. Supposedly, it was part of the Fallen's curse; black wings and a smoky smell which distinguished them from the regular Angels.

Soon, Ethon whispered gently into my ear, "It's okay to come out from there." He gently nudged my cheek with his nose. "Let me see those beautiful eyes."

I slowly moved my head back, tracing his strong jawline with my lips – *What was I doing?* - until met his handsome face, inches from mine. His eyes sparkled in different hues of garnet. They were a very dark red, with specks of bright ruby. The colors almost seemed to be swirling together. I blinked, thinking my eyes were playing tricks on me, but when I opened them again, it was the same. The color in his eyes was definitely swirling.

"What's wrong?" He asked, narrowing his eyes at me.

"Your eyes are very...different."

"Different, as in creepy?"

"No. Not creepy. They're actually very beautiful."

He chuckled. "Well that's the first time they've ever been called beautiful. They're part of the curse."

"Well, they're original, I'll give you that. Did you know the colors in your eyes swirl together?"

He grinned. "Yes, but that's nothing. Wait until you see what happens when I get pissed off."

"Flames?" I asked, jokingly.

"You've seen them?" His brow furrowed.

"Are you serious? I was just kidding," I exhaled.

He shrugged. "You know that red is a power color? It's also the color of lust," he noted.

I narrowed my eyes at him. "So I've heard. But don't think you can seduce me with your wit and charms, devil boy."

Ethon looked like he took my words as a personal challenge. "Don't underestimate me, Nephilim. You have no idea what I'm capable of. My wit and charm are only a small fragment of the powers I've been bestowed. Plus, I have the bond in my favor." His

47

eyes suddenly turned a totally different red. An almost fiery red, swirling with orange and yellow hues.

"What?" I gasped.

His grin grew into a huge smile. "Hang on. Here we go," he warned, taking a nose dive into a forest of tall spruce trees.

I screamed as we rolled a few times, and then evened out. He zoomed in and around of the forest like nothing. With a flip, he instantly turned on his back, and I was now laying on top of him, watching everything zoom past us in a blur.

"Ethon!" I shrieked.

He was too amused for my liking.

Turning back over, I heard, "We're almost there."

"Where?"

"My place."

"Your place?"

"Yes. Do you see that huge birch tree ahead?"

"Yes," I answered.

"Well, we need to go through it."

"What do you mean 'go through it'?" My heart started to race. We were heading straight for the huge trunk, and weren't slowing down.

"Holy crap!" I shouted.

What if he was a total kamikaze kind of Fallen Angel?

I'd heard about crazy people going off the deep end from jealousy. This bond was nothing to mess with. I just hoped Ethon wasn't the type who thought 'if you aren't mine, you will be no one else's.' That would totally suck.

"What the hell are you doing?" I gasped.

"Don't you trust me?" He laughed.

"Maybe," I said desperately, hoping not to anger him. In response, he flew faster.

We were going to hit the damn tree. I closed my eyes and braced for impact.

Three...two...one...

"Emma. We're here," Ethon said softly.

"What?" I peeled my face from his shoulder and opened my eyes. We were in a completely different place. It was bright and sunny. Almost like a painting.

It was a large area filled with the greenest grass. In the center of this oasis, a solitary willow stood on the edge of a large pond. Its long branches hung low, dipping into the water's edge.

Behind the tree, in the distance, was a grassy hill. Ethon flew us to the highest point and set us down carefully. He paused and I suddenly realized I hadn't released my talon-like grip. I quickly let go and stepped back, watching his beautiful black wings fold behind his back and disappear. I shook my head, still amazed by the hidden wings. That would still take some getting used to.

"What is this place?" I asked.

"It's a place my father gifted to me after my transformation - a portal to my own little world. No one knows about it, except me and father. It was something special he created just for me. A place I could go to if I ever felt in danger, or just needed to get away from the bullshit of the Underworld. Sometimes I wish I could stay here forever."

"Why don't you?" I asked.

"Because, believe it or not, my father needs me."

I smiled. "That's really awesome, but also hard to comprehend, him being the all-powerful Ruler of the Underworld and all."

Ethon nodded. "He does have a mean streak, but also another side, which no one sees but me. He'd never *dare* show that side to any of his Fallen. It's part of the job. He has to be a hard ass with them to maintain order. It's challenging to rule a bunch of lazy, drunken immortals."

"But growing up, when it was just me and him in his chambers alone, it was a whole different story. I was the recipient to the one, small part of his heart that could love."

"I could tell. The way he looked at you," I said, remembering the way he interacted with Ethon. But none of that changed how I felt about Lucifer. I didn't trust him. The only reason he agreed to help us was for his own selfish reasons. He wanted to get back at Lucian for coming against him. It was payback, and we were the vehicle. Plus, his involvement came with a high price - a soul. There was no good in that. Just pure evil.

"You alright?" Ethon said, snapping me from my ill thoughts.

"Yes, I'm fine."

"You're the first person I've brought here," he said with a gleam in his eye.

"Really? That's sort of hard to believe."

"What's so hard to believe?"

"Weren't you Hell's most eligible bachelor?"

Ethon laughed out loud. "I wish. There aren't too many available

Fallen women, and you don't want to be around the ones who are. Trust me," he shivered.

"Not your type?"

"Let's just say that they could all be paired with Bane or Azzah."

"Oh," I giggled.

"So, it's no surprise that when I saw your beautiful face, I was instantly enchanted," he said.

I felt a heat rush through my cheeks.

"Before I laid eyes on you, I could feel something. It was the strangest feeling, like an electrical current humming in the air around me. I started to feel lightheaded, and my heart began to race. Then, when I stepped into the room, I was slammed with reality. You were standing there. The most beautiful creature I'd ever laid eyes on. I couldn't comprehend what was happening until we touched, and I was instantly bewitched."

"Ethon—"

"You must have felt the same thing, right?" he asked.

I paused, and then nodded.

"Why don't we take a walk down to the pond? We can talk on the way," he suggested.

I glanced at him with a raised eyebrow. "You're not going to fly us?"

"No. We have a lot of time to kill, and walking would be good. Plus, I need to cool down from having you so close."

My face flushed with heat again. "So, is the time in this place like time in the Underworld? Is a day in here, a week or two out there?"

"No, but I wish it was. That would totally piss some people off," he laughed.

"Yes, and that would be a very bad thing," I said.

"So, walk with me?" he held out his hand and I took it. We were instantly jolted again with that familiar electrical buzz and magnetism. Slowly we made our way down the hill.

"I could totally get used to this," he said.

"I'm sure you could," I answered.

SIX

"I'M CURIOUS AS TO WHY the bond chose us, and really want to know more about you. Would you care to enlighten me about your life?"

"You mean from the beginning?" I questioned.

"Sure, or wherever you'd like to start."

"Well, I recently found out that my mom and dad weren't my real parents. I had been given to them at birth, as protection from of Lucian's attempt to eradicate all Nephilim."

"And your adopted parents were good to you?"

"I never knew I was adopted. They loved me like I was their own, and I never felt as if I wasn't theirs. I never once questioned it. They were amazing, and I loved them so much."

"What happened to them?" he questioned.

My breath momentarily seized in my throat. I inhaled deeply

and continued.

"We were on our way home driving on a dark road when one of Lucian's Fallen dropped down from the sky, right in front of our car. My dad swerved to avoid him, and we careened off the road, straight into some trees. Kade saved me. He was my Guardian, and had followed behind us in another car. Somehow, before the impact, he managed to get into our car and shield me from the crash. I had been screaming, so he put me to sleep." My heart ached as I thought about it. "If it could have been possible, he would've saved my parents, but there was only time to save one. And I was his priority. They were killed instantly."

"I'm so sorry," he said softly.

"Thank you," I said.

"So this Kade is a true hero," he said with a hint of sarcasm.

"Yes. He is a hero. My hero. He saved me more times than I can count, and I don't appreciate you degrading his actions."

"Hey, I'm not here to start a war. I really am grateful he saved you, but that doesn't mean we will be buddies. Right now your hero is my enemy. He holds the heart of the girl I've bonded too. You have to remember, I never chose this. In a split second, the bond ripped out half of my heart and handed it to you. Hell if *I'm* going to stand by and let someone steal that part from me. I am here for you, Emma, and you alone. I will protect you and keep you safe, because fate has chosen us to be together."

I closed my eyes and shook my head. "I realize that, and I'm sorry. But you also have to remember it wasn't my decision either. This damn bond, or fate, or whatever the hell you immortals call it, really screwed up my life. I never asked to be bonded to anyone, let alone two completely different people. I'm the one who will have to make a choice and break someone's heart. It's a pressure I don't want, or need."

"Fair enough. Let's change the subject," he said. "I was told how your Guardian became mortal...but I'm confused as to why he hasn't sealed the bond with you yet?"

"How the hell would you know? Maybe he did," I said. I didn't like him talking negative about Kade, or our relationship. He had no clue what we'd been through.

"Oh, I'd know. If he sealed the bond, I wouldn't be in the middle of this damn dilemma."

"Well, you'll have to deal with it. He has been doing his job and looking out for my best interests, not his own. Kade is a gentleman, and keeps in line with my wishes."

Ethon huffed, "Do-gooder."

"Hero," I replied.

He snickered. "About heroes, word is you slayed our Hellhounds. Is this true?"

"I did." I kept a straight face because I didn't want him to think I was weak.

"And how the hell did you do that?"

"Magic," I said flatly, then grinned.

"Alright. I'll give you that. You are pretty magical," he agreed. "I raised a few of those Hellhounds myself. They were practically family and would tear anyone's head off who got near."

I glared at him. "Your 'dogs' killed a friend of mine, and nearly killed the rest of us. They deserved their end."

"They were only doing their job," he stated.

"So was I, and I don't have one ounce of regret," I said raising my voice an octave louder.

His eyes glazed over. "I think you and I are more alike than you think."

"How would you know?" I questioned.

"Because when those you care about are in danger, you wouldn't hesitate to kill for them, and in the end you have no regrets."

I nodded. He was right. That *was* exactly how I felt.

A few weeks ago, I would rather have captured a bug and set it free, than killed it. Now, I was battling with supernatural beings, killing when I had the chance. It made me wonder what my future had in store. What would I become? I could feel a change happening. If I had a moment of peace, it would probably scare the hell out of me. Instead, the threat of constant danger strengthened and protected me from my weaker self.

"My father should make you a Gatekeeper," he snickered.

"Screw that. He can guard his own damn gates."

"Feisty. I like that," he noted with a wicked grin.

I shook my head and grinned back. He was right. This was not my normal temperament. He was bringing out a different side of me...and I sort of liked it.

"What's your story, Ethon? I'll bet you were a little devil growing up..." I sniggered at my amusing word play.

"Oh, the shame, Emma. That was pretty bad," he said shaking

his head. "But seriously, you want to hear my story?"

"Yes. I've been told we have some time to kill. So, I know the story of how you ended up with Lucifer, but what was it like growing up in hell?"

"Fair warning, my story is pretty boring. The Underworld probably wasn't much different than growing up in any other place, except it was dark, hot, and there weren't many others to interact with. I spent a lot of time either with my father, his pets, or those who schooled and trained me. That two-headed mutt you met was one of my best friends."

"I could tell it, or they, really loved you," I giggled.

"Yeah, it wasn't a charmed life, but it wasn't boring. My father kept me hidden deep within his chambers for safety's sake, because he knew Lucian would have me killed if he ever found out. He had his best warriors train me in every aspect of battle. When I turned eighteen, my transformation gifted me wings and speed, and ever since, there has been no one who can match me." His lips turned up slightly.

"After I turned eighteen, my father set me free. I was stronger than any of his best warriors, and he knew I could take care of myself. I've been free ever since."

I exhaled into a whistle. "That wasn't boring. It sounds like you've led a very adventurous life."

"I don't know if you'd call it 'adventurous', but I see your point. It wasn't boring."

We finally reached the weeping willow, and Ethon sat under the shade of its hanging branches. The pond was the most beautiful turquoise blue. He took a small pebble and skipped it across the top of the water, sending ripples out to all its corners.

"Come. Sit," he said, patting the ground next to him.

I slowly made my way over and settled into a spot near him, but not *too* close.

"So what is the connection you have with Alaine?" he questioned.

I paused before I answered because I knew he wasn't supposed to know Alaine was my birth mother.

He already knew Samuel was my father. If he found out Alaine was my birth mother, things would get complicated very quickly. I just hoped he wouldn't put two-and-two together. Right now, he thought I was a Nephilim - half-mortal and half-immortal, and my birth mother was human. So that would count Alaine out. I'd just leave the explaining of that particular part of my life to Samuel and Alaine, when the time was right.

"Well, Alaine is my mother's half-sister, and the only living kin I have left. As soon as she heard about the accident and subsequent death of my parents, she immediately made arrangements, and took me in."

"That was very generous of her. She seems like a very caring woman. And what about the other two mortals? How did she come by them?"

"Well, Courtney and Caleb were children of her best friend who died of cancer. Alaine was with her just before she died, and promised her she'd take care of them. They've been with her since."

Ethon nodded. "That was a very brave thing to do, to rear another's children. I have great respect for your aunt."

"So do I," I whispered. I scooted forward until I almost touched his leg, because it felt like there was something uneven under me. When I looked back, I noticed a perfectly square rock under the earth. Ethon's arm quickly snaked around my waist, and pulled me in-between his legs, with my back resting on his chest.

"Are you more comfortable now?" he asked.

My pulse began to race, and my stomach twisted. "Yes," I gulped.

I didn't want to turn around because I knew if I did, I would be in trouble. The pull of the bond was just too strong.

I felt his large hands engulf my waist, and then was lifted and turned like I weighed nothing. I was now face to face with the deviled beauty, straddling him. His crimson eyes were ablaze with desire, and this time I could see little specks, or embers, burning deep within them. I was completely spellbound.

"You're beautiful," he exhaled. "Sinfully beautiful." His fingers grazed the side of my cheek, leaving a trail of tingles.

"Ethon, what are you doing?"

"I think if you're going to have to make a decision about one of us, I should at least get a chance to show you what I have to offer. Don't you think that's only fair?"

"Yes," I automatically said, "I mean, no... I – I don't know." There was a war going on inside of myself, and he could see it.

"Don't worry. I promise not to seal any bonds," he assured me with a grin on his face. And then I *thought* I heard him whisper. "But we might get close."

His arms suddenly wrapped around me. Electricity buzzed

heavily, causing everything to melt away, except…I was hyper-aware of where our bodies touched. His eyes were fire, burning even brighter. They locked me in and took me captive.

Before I could blink, he pressed his warm lips to mine, and I melted against his large frame.

"Ethon," I whispered into his mouth. The heat between us was growing, we were nearly combustible.

"I've got you," he said, out of breath. He then rolled us backwards, his body stretching out on top of mine. Holding my arms above my head with one hand, he slowly left open kisses on the nape of my neck, across my jawline, and then back to my lips. I moaned with pleasure as his eager mouth found mine.

It happened so fast, but it felt so damn good.

I was warring with myself. We should stop, it wasn't fair to Kade. But the bond wanted us to seal its magic. It was strong and tenacious, attempting to block all rational.

A cacophonous shrill suddenly pierced the air.

I opened my eyes.

Soaring high above, was a large black raven. It's ungodly, shrieking caw persisted, completely terminating our heated make-out session.

Ethon pushed himself up and yelled, "Ash, you stupid-ass bird. I'll pluck out your freaking feathers out – one by one - until you're naked, and then I'll cook and eat you!"

The huge bird started to descend from the sky, and as it did, I sat up and tried to straighten myself. I had a disturbing feeling that Lucifer might have been watching us through his dark villainous eyes. I wondered how long he was above us, or how much it heard.

Ash finally flapped down and landed on a branch, just out of reach. Its head tilted back and forth, and its beady black eyes steeled on us.

"Father? Are you here?" Ethon asked the bird.

The raven gave a slight nod of its head. At least it looked like a nod.

"How the hell did you find me here?" Ethon yelled at it.

It flapped its wings a few times, and then floated down until it sat right next to him. Suddenly its beak began to move and intelligible words emerged. The voice was unmistakable. It was Lucifer.

I felt embarrassed he'd seen us.

"Ethon. Bane and Azzah are searching for you. The Darkling sent by Lucian have been exterminated, and the girl must be returned. You do not need a war with the Guardians on your hands. It will only complicate matters."

"You know I could give a shit," Ethon answered.

"Ethon," Lucifer scolded. "You have an abundance of time to seal the bond. Now is not the time. Not while we are in the midst of war."

"I'm fully aware, and we weren't going to seal any bond," he answered.

"Lucian was testing the strength of the Guardians. He is gathering an army and building his power, biding his time until he strikes. My army is ready and awaiting orders. But a word of caution. Lucian is sly. He is watching from the shadows. Be on your guard at all times, my son. He would revel in killing you and presenting me your head on a platter."

"Don't be concerned about me, father. I can take care of myself."

"I trust in you, but a father worries. Take her back, Ethon. Bane and Azzah are nearby."

"I will."

The raven gave one more piercing shrill and took off. I watched it fly toward an almost invisible spiral in the sky, and then it vanished.

Ethon huffed, then stood and brushed himself off. "Well, that freaking sucked. I'm sorry we were so rudely interrupted."

"I'm sort of glad we were. I think we needed it... we probably would not have stopped."

His eyes snapped to mine and beamed. "I knew you couldn't resist my charms."

I opened my mouth, but nothing came out. He was right. His charms were almost impossible to resist, even without the bond. The bond just multiplied it one thousand times.

We may have been complete opposites, but I kind of liked who I was around him. I had previously thought choosing was going to be really simple. Ethon wasn't even on my radar until today. I couldn't say that now. He was a spitfire, and very witty. He'd also endured his own battles, and was raised by someone other than his birth parents. Thankfully, Lucifer saved him and kept him safe. He was all that remained of his bloodline.

Then, there was Kade...who was everything I'd ever dreamed about in a guy. He was the very first boy to steal my heart. A knight in shining armor. The bond chose us first, and I knew why. Kade had many good qualities. He was handsome, sweet, protective, a perfect gentleman, and he had his own spunk and charm. Most importantly, he had validated his love for me over and over again.

"Are you ready?" Ethon asked, stepping closer.

"Yes." The air around us was alive and buzzing.

"Let's fly, angel," he smiled, holding his hand out to me. I giggled, placing my hand in his. Ethon yanked me to him, wrapping his arms around me. I decided to hook my legs around his waist...for safety reasons.

He gave me one last kiss.

"Hold on," he whispered. His beautiful wings magically appeared and stretched out past his sides.

I tightened my hold on his neck and waist, and a look of pleasure washed over his face. He lifted his eyes to the sky, and with a flap of his wings, we shot up. I knew we probably wouldn't have any more alone time, but I was glad I had a chance to learn a little about him.

We were flying in the same direction Ash had flown. I twisted my head up just to see if I could see anything, and noticed a small ripple in the sky.

As soon as we reached it, we were instantly transported from bright and sunny, to the dark forest, dodging trees. Ethon was flying so fast, everything was a blur. It made me nauseated. Closing my eyes, I burrowed my face into his neck and breathed in his calming scent.

"Please let me know when I can open my eyes again," I murmured against his skin.

"Deal," he chuckled.

SEVEN

THERE WAS A SUDDEN CHANGE in direction, and I knew we were headed straight up. I quickly opened my eyes to peek, just as we burst from the darkness of the trees, into the dark open sky. Ahead of us, about a half-mile away, two dark figures were headed toward us. The goons.

Bane and Azzah looked just as excited to see us as we were to see them. Their faces were hard, and had Darkling blood splattered all over. They looked like the most miserable creatures on the planet. *Were they ever in a good mood?*

I had a sneaking suspicion that Bane and Azzah were bitter to the core; it exuded from their pores. Anger and hate flowed through their veins.

"So, did we have fun slaying the Darkling?" Ethon jested.

They growled in response, glares were evil, and their faces

started to turn a shade of red.

"Ethon, don't," I pleaded. I knew he had a love-hate relationship with them, but I was on a hate-hate basis with them right now. He was making it worse.

He glanced at me with a nod, as if he was complying.

"They're all dead," Bane said in a deep voice. "Samuel wants the girl."

"I know. We were just on our way back."

"We'll escort you," Azzah said. His voice low and showed no emotion.

"If you can catch me," Ethon antagonized.

Flapping his wings, we shot off. I screamed and burrowed into him again, as he flew at a crazy supersonic speed. I knew we lost Bane and Azzah and I was pretty happy about it.

A little over a minute later his cheek pressed on mine. "We're here."

As I opened my eyes, Alaine's house came into view. It was a beautiful site from the air, except the Labyrinth. There, the ground was covered with death.

A small crowd was gathered out by the cabin in the back, and Ethon chose to land directly in the center.

Dammit.

My stomach churned as we made our descent.

As soon as our feet touched the ground, Alaine ran and grabbed me, pulling me into her embrace, away from Ethon.

"Oh my God, Emma, are you okay?" She questioned, checking me over. Samuel also came and wrapped his arms around me.

"Yes, I'm fine," I answered.

I didn't want to raise my head because Kade and Ethon were on either side of us.

Alaine paused and walked me toward the house, in Kade's direction. Her arm was still cradled around me.

"Are you okay?" Kade asked. His hazel eyes focused on me, pulling me back into his world. I knew his words had more meaning behind them. He wanted to know if Ethon hurt me, or sealed the bond.

"Yes, I'm fine. Nothing happened," I answered, reassuring him.

I was really glad that Ash showed up when he did. He saved us.

Kade nodded and his face instantly washed with relief. "Good," he breathed, and then glared behind me at Ethon.

"I'll talk to you later, okay?" I said softly.

"Okay," he answered, lifting his fingers to graze my face.

The bond with Kade was still as strong as it was with Ethon. It was just that Kade is a bit more restrained with our intimacy. However, I knew if the chance presented itself, he would willingly unbridle his passion, and we could easily get into a lot of trouble. Bond-sealing kind of trouble.

I was trapped. Tethered between two hearts. Both wanting nothing more than to love and protect me. That's why the bonds were created. For two separate beings to find their one true love, spending the rest of eternity making each other happy.

Whoever was in charge of dishing out my Immortal Bonds, must have been really drunk.

At first I didn't understand the influence of the Immortal Bond, but I was starting to find out firsthand how powerful it really was. Most mortals would mistakenly call it insta-love or just plain lust, but the Immortal bond far surpassed any reason. It was magical. It was something so mysterious and so complex. A conjoining of two fated hearts, destined for each other, finally finding their perfect companion. A single touch connected them, and at that moment, the pull of the bond was unyielding, and only upon consummation, would the bond be sealed. Two hearts would be bound in an enchanted love, devotion, and burning passion, which would last for all eternity. It was beautiful, yet indescribable and unexplainable, specifically designed by the creator himself.

"Is everyone alright?" I asked her.

"Yes. Thomas was the only one who sustained an injury. A blade to his thigh. He's already been bandaged up and is resting."

"How many Darkling were there?" I asked.

"At least five dozen," Samuel answered.

"How many Darkling are there?"

"More than we can count," he said.

"We defeated these, and that's all that matters. Lucian knows how strong we are, and it will take him some time to regroup, which is good, because your friends arrive tomorrow," Alaine said.

Crap on a stick.

I'd completely forgotten my friends were coming to visit me… for four days.

God would surely have to help us.

EIGHT

W HEN WE REACHED THE DOOR to go inside, Samuel stopped.

"Aren't you coming?" I asked.

"I've decided to stay in the cottage so Alaine can place the protective barrier around the house."

"But you won't be protected," I said.

"Don't worry about me. I've spent the majority of my life surviving without a barrier. I'll be fine."

I turned and gave him a hug, and he warmly returned my embrace. It was so good to see him again.

"How are your wings?" I questioned, hoping they were doing better.

"I think they should be ready to fly in a few weeks. I hope."

"Really? That's awesome."

"How are you holding up?" he asked.

I assumed he meant the situation with Kade and Ethon.

"I'm holding it all together for now," I sadly grinned.

"Well, if you ever break, Alaine and I are always here to help mend the pieces."

That was pretty deep. "Thank you," I breathed. "I appreciate that."

He smiled and gave me one last squeeze before heading back toward the boys. I think the only positive of the quest into the Underworld was getting to know Samuel. The man who made up half of my genetics. The whole journey brought us closer, and gave me a deep respect and love for him.

I glanced back and noticed Ethon was gone. He must have returned to the tower, and I didn't blame him. He was outnumbered by a bunch of Guardians who were itching to send him back to Hell.

I had eight more months to survive before my transformation, and it seemed like an eternity away. I just hoped whenever Lucian decided to attack, Lucifer would keep his end of the deal, and we would be rid of him once and for all.

But the thought of Lucifer taking someone's soul, in return for his allegiance, made me sick. I wouldn't allow him to do it. When the time came, I would simply do whatever it took to keep everyone safe. But, I wouldn't think about that right now. I had to focus on keeping Jeremy and Lia safe for the next four days.

"So where did Ethon take you?" Alaine asked.

"He took me to a safe place, almost like a porthole, but when we entered it was like a little oasis. It was beautiful."

"Was he a gentleman?" She asked. She didn't look at me but

kept her eyes forward as we walked. I knew she was performing her motherly duty, and could tell she felt a bit uncomfortable asking.

"Yes. Yes, he was. We mostly talked, and you were right. He's not such a bad person."

She smiled and nodded. I could tell she was relieved.

I knew deep inside she didn't want to have Lucifer as an in-law. Hell, I didn't want that either. He wasn't exactly someone you wanted passing dinner rolls across the family dining table.

"Well that's good. I'm glad you're okay. Courtney was looking for you. She's a bit shaken up by the whole battle. Maybe you can go and give her some comfort?"

"Of course," I answered. "I promised her I would hang out with her today. I'll go check on her now."

"That would be nice. Thank you, Emma." She gave me a hug before we parted ways. She went into her study, and I went upstairs to my room.

My mind was swirling, thinking about my mini adventure with Ethon. I closed my eyes, and his face was there. Clear as day. His eyes burning bright with passion.

My heart started to race.

No! I can't do this. I just can't.

I felt like I was betraying Kade, but then again, we were never official. I knew the way Kade felt about me, and how I felt about him, but I still wanted to keep myself neutral. I didn't want to deal with the pressure of bonding, dammit.

The decision I'd have to make would be permanent, as in the one I would have to live with for the rest of my immortal life. I wasn't going to be impulsive or rush into anything.

Yeah, easier said than done.

I knew they wouldn't relent. Each one had a point to prove. Which made me wonder, would the man I didn't choose be stuck alone forever? Okay, I'm putting pressure on myself again.

I just needed to make sure they didn't kill each other before I made my choice. Thank God I had Alaine and Samuel here with me. I needed to get one of those chastity belts. The metal ones with a lock and key. Heck, if I told them about my idea, they'd probably order one immediately.

Then again, all of this worrying would be for nothing if I didn't even make it to my eighteenth birthday.

I sighed and continued up the stairs.

As I turned down the hallway toward my bedroom, I noticed Courtney's door was open. I decided to walk down and see if she was okay.

"Hello?" I called.

"Who is it?"

"Emma."

"Come in, Emma," she answered. "I'm in the closet."

I walked in, toward her closet. The light was on, and inside was Courtney, sitting on pile of pillows with books surrounding her. There was also a plate with two muffins. One was half eaten.

"What are you doing in here?" I asked.

"Reading," she answered flatly.

"Why in the closet?"

"The closet is a place I feel safe from danger."

"It is?" I questioned.

"Yes. When Caleb and I were younger, our mother told us that if we ever felt afraid, the safest place was in the closet. She even painted the inside of mine with pretty flowers. Whenever I was scared, she would turn on the light, bring pillows and blankets inside, and read me stories until I fell asleep. Ever since then, it's been my safe place."

"That's awesome, Courtney. May I join you?"

"Of course. To be honest, I think you need this place more than I do."

"I think you're right. Maybe I'll just hide out with you until I turn eighteen."

"You're funny," she giggled. "When do you turn eighteen?"

"In about eight months."

"Well, you are welcome to use my safe place whenever you want. Actually, you can just use your own. Being in a smaller space, surrounded by things you love, really helps whenever you're afraid. That's why I have all my books in here."

"I'll definitely keep that in mind," I smiled.

The second I stepped inside her closet the outside world did seem to disappear. Courtney was a small reminder of how it felt to be human. We laughed, talked about our parents, played a few card games, ate candy, and drank soda. It seemed like forever since I had fun like that.

"We need to do this more often," I said, finally getting to take my leave.

"Yes, we should. Even though I'm only thirteen, I'm still fun."

"Yeah, you are. You're practically my little sister," I noted.

"I am?" Her face lit up like the sun.

"Well, we're both being raised by Alaine, so that means we're related."

"I like that. I like the idea of having you as a big sister."

"I like it too. Hey, you'll get a chance to meet my best friends. They're coming tomorrow to visit from LA. I think they'll really get along with you and Caleb."

"Alaine is letting your friends come here?" Her eyes widened with concern.

"Yes, but they're only staying for four days, and we have to make sure they stay inside. I'll need you and Caleb to help me keep them busy. They love to watch movies."

"Oh, I have loads of movies."

"Awesome. And they love to play board games too."

Courtney's face lit up and she even squealed a bit, because she also loved them.

My job was done here, and I felt good about it.

"See you later alligator."

She giggled. "Not for a while crocodile."

NINE

WHEN I STEPPED INTO MY room, sitting on the desk were the gifts from Kade. I breathed deep to prepare myself and walked over to them. I lifted the cover of my mother's jewelry box first, and left it open.

Holding the box of pictures, I walked over to my bed, grabbed a pillow, and headed over to my closet. I clicked on the light, dropped my pillow down, and sat in the middle of the floor. Over the next few hours, I relived wonderful memories, and fell asleep crying. My pillow was soaked with tears.

A rapping at the door woke me.

Popping up I realized I was still in my closet. I didn't even know if it was morning or night. I glanced at the clock and it was after 7:00 pm. My eyes were swollen and my head was pounding.

"Who is it?" I asked. My voice cracked and was weak.

"Prince Charming?" the voice answered, as if it wasn't sure of the answer.

I paused and smiled, then walked over and unlocked the door.

Kade stood there with a plate of spaghetti, garlic bread, and a tossed salad.

"You didn't show at dinner, so I asked Alaine if I could bring you a plate. She gave the okay, but also said she'd be watching. I can almost feel her eyes on my back."

I laughed. "Come in." Taking the plate, I walked over to my desk and set it down. "Thank you for bringing the boxes here."

"I actually gave them to Alaine. She's the one who brought them in."

He paused at the closet. I watched his eyes glance over the dampened pillow and pictures spread out all over the floor. "I'm sorry if you weren't ready for them."

I walked past the bathroom door and noticed my face in the mirror. My eyes were bloodshot and my nose was bright red.

"I don't know if I would ever be ready for them, but I needed it. I miss them so much. Looking through the pictures almost brought them back to life again. I relived all the wonderful memories I had with them."

Kade smiled and walked over to me. He stood inches away, making my stomach twist. "I'm sorry I let you leave with him. I should have kept you with me. I could have kept you safe."

"It's okay. I was safe. You did what you thought was best. I appreciate that."

"Where did he take you?"

I wasn't going to lie to him. He didn't deserve that.

"He took me to a secret place of his, and we stayed there until it was safe to leave."

"How did you know when to leave?"

"The raven, Ash, told us. Well, it wasn't really the raven, it was Lucifer talking through it."

He hesitated. I could see he wanted to ask me something.

"What is it?" I asked.

"Did he try anything?"

"We mostly talked, but...he did kiss me."

Kade's eyes shut, and he took in a deep breath.

"That was it. Nothing else happened. I promise," I assured him.

"I'm not mad at you. I know the power of the bond, but knowing that bastard's lips touched yours, makes my blood boil. You're better than him, Emma. You deserve so much better than the Underworld. Do you think Lucifer will ever allow you to live a happy life?"

He seemed truly vexed. "One day he will find out who you truly are, and so will Ethon. Then, they will stop at nothing to make you theirs. If you think Lucian is bad, remember that Lucifer created him. His power is small in comparison."

"Lucifer could have crushed Lucian long ago, but he has a reason for every action or inaction. He takes joy in watching others suffer. Lucian defied him and he will pay dearly before his end. This is the only reason Lucifer agreed to help. I just want you to be aware of what he really is. Don't be deceived. Ethon is also not what he seems. Just remember where he came from." He placed his hand on the side of my cheek, and I took hold of it. "Please be safe and smart around him."

He lifted my chin, then leaned down and kissed me lightly. "I'll see you tomorrow," he said, then turned and left the room.

My head was spinning. I was slowly going crazy, and was never more thankful that Jeremy and Lia were coming tomorrow. I needed sanity back in my life.

TEN

I COULDN'T SLEEP. TOSSING AND turning, my mind flashed back and forth between Kade and Ethon, my parents, Samuel and Alaine, and Lucian and Lucifer. Each one had a part they were playing in my life, whether I liked it or not.

In a few short hours I'd get to see my best friends, and couldn't wait to see their faces. I needed to have a bit of familiarity back in my life. Maybe they could help me sort through all this madness. But how could they when they weren't allowed to know about my new hidden world?

There had to be something done about all the Guardians in the house. They would instantly know something was up when they saw six *perfect* guys living under one roof. Lia wouldn't mind because she would be dazed by all the hotness, but Jeremy was a different story. He would analyze everything, wondering why they were here. He would ask one million questions, I couldn't answer.

Finally giving up on sleep, I dragged myself from my bed and pulled back the curtains to watch the sun rise. It was beautiful. Such a difference from yesterday. The clouds looked as if they were painted across the sky in beautiful shades of lavender and pink.

After I changed and put on some make-up, I headed downstairs. Alaine had everyone gathered in the main area at the bottom of the stairs, going over the final plans for the next four days.

"Why aren't they flying into Fairbanks? It'd be so much faster to get them from there," Caleb asked from the top of the stairs. I glanced over to him. I hadn't seen him since I'd left for the Underworld, and I was glad to see he was looking healthy.

He glanced at me and smiled.

"It is closer to us, but Fairbanks is a place where Fallen and Darkling are known to hang out. There is a much greater chance of being attacked if we go up there. The Fallen don't like places that are heavily populated, so Anchorage is the safer route, even if it takes hours to get there."

Per Alaine's instructions, we were taking two cars. Dominic would be driving Malachi, me, and Kade. And Samuel would be driving the second car with Ethon and his goons. This was just to make sure we were fully protected. The second car wasn't supposed to be seen.

Only Kade, Dominic, and Malachi were allowed to be shown or present for the next four days. This was to minimize any unnecessary questions. If questions did arise, they were relatives visiting for a week.

It seemed like an eternity since I'd last seen my friends. My life had changed so much, and I wondered if they would notice the change in me. I could not only feel it, I could see it when I looked in the mirror. The trip into the Underworld stripped most my humanity. I was different on the inside. Stronger. Braver. But still in pieces. I knew it would eventually heal and come together, but it just wouldn't be anytime soon.

Jeremy and Lia were very fragile. They didn't like scary things, and I knew I'd have to keep them close at all times. They probably thought they were coming up to explore the Last Frontier, but the exploration would mainly be in Alaine's home. Maybe a few other places close by.

I was glad to have Ethon's backup. Maybe, because he was here, Jeremy and Lia could still have a safe, eventful trip.

After Alaine's debriefing, we all had breakfast, and then left on our long journey to the airport.

The lack of sleep was catching up to me, and Kade, being as perceptive as always, wrapped his arm around me. I laid my head on his shoulder and felt his warm lips on top of my head. He left them there, breathing in my scent. It wasn't long before I fell fast asleep.

It felt like I'd just closed my eyes when I was nudged awake. I opened my eyes, and we were already at the airport.

"Whoa. I knocked out."

"Yeah you did," Kade whispered.

"What pretty boy here failed to mention is that you snored. A lot," Dominic said loudly.

"No way. I don't snore," I huffed.

"Well, you kind of did, but it wasn't loud," Kade tried to assure me.

"Hell, yes it was," Dom asserted, twisting his head back. "Damn Emma, you were snoring like a drunken sailor."

"Shut up! I was not!" I blushed.

Malachi chuckled.

"Malachi, was I snoring?" I asked.

"Yes, but it was kinda cute," he said.

"There is no such thing as a cute snore," I mumbled from beneath the hands covering my face.

"Yeah, thank God for the music. It drowned out most of your horn blowing," Dom added.

I gasped, hiding my face in Kade's shoulder. "Kill me...just make it fast. If you loved me, you'd put me out of my misery."

"Oh, come on now, you know I tell it like it is," I hear from the front seat. I looked up in time to see Dom wiggling his eyebrows at me in the rear-view mirror.

Kade came to my rescue.

"We should start heading in. They land in about ten minutes."

Three of us would be going inside, and Dominic would be staying.

As we started to head into the terminal, I noticed the other black Hummer parked across the lot. I knew Ethon was inside, watching. It made my insides twist, and made me feel a bit nervous. This was a completely new emotion. I'd never had the affection of two different boys.

Kade took hold of my hand and laced his fingers in mine. Perfect fit. As always.

Malachi quickly took his position on the other side of me.

As we walked into the airport I had a sudden feeling of déjà vu. It wasn't long ago I was here, with Kade and Malachi on either side of me, walking through this very place. I thought back and remembered how clueless and hopeless I was. I had been in pieces, damaged, weak, and vulnerable.

"You alright?" Kade whispered in my ear. The warmth of his breath caressed my cheek, soothing my growing anxieties.

"Yes, just having an unpleasant flashback," I replied.

He wrapped his arm around me, pulling me closer. He never failed to comfort me.

"Well, I should warn you here and now – I'm not allowing you to use the bathrooms here."

"Don't worry. I'm never, ever using another airport bathroom again," I promised.

He laughed, and his laughter made me laugh. I loved being around him. He brought out the best in me. I could completely be myself, and he still loved every part of me, including my snoring, unfortunate Hell-smell, or even my ugly cry face. Now that meant something.

There was no trouble as we made our way in. The air was clear of stench, except for a large woman who walked by, crop-dusted with her old lady perfume. It was so pungent and thick I felt like I was chewing it.

We made our way to the information board and confirmed their flight had just landed.

Kade and I made our way up the escalator to greet them, while Malachi stayed down near baggage claim.

It seemed forever before we started to see signs of arriving passengers making their way toward us. My stomach twisted with anticipation, I couldn't keep still.

"I'm going to stand over there," Kade said, pointing to a column a few feet behind us.

"You can stay here with me," I smiled. "They won't bite."

He raised an eyebrow.

"Okay, maybe Lia will, but it's not her fault. Have you seen your ass?"

"Well, in that case, I'll park it against the column," he laughed.

God he was gorgeous. His hair was disheveled to perfection, and I just noticed how he was wearing nicely fitted blue jeans, and a light gray sweater. His hazel eyes seemed to mimic the gray, but were swirled with green, blue, and flecks of yellow.

"What?" he grinned.

I blushed, knowing I had been checking him out a little too long. "Oh nothing. You just look really – nice," I said nodding my head in approval.

"Thanks," he gleamed. Then he pivoted and walked toward the column dramatically swaying his hips back and forth drawing attention to his rear.

I laughed out loud, and my heart filled with warmth. *He was something else.*

As soon as I turned my head, a familiar face rounded the corner, followed by a high-piercing scream. Lia bounded down the hall with her arms spread out like an eagle. Her large, pink backpack bounced up and down on her back, making her run completely awkward.

"Emma!" she screamed.

"Lia," I called back, and ran to meet her.

We almost fell as we crashed together and hugged, spinning in circles.

"Oh my God. You are alive. And you look...you look like you just woke up," she said, as we stopped. I had to blink a couple of times because even though we had stopped, the world around us hadn't.

I laughed. "You are correct. I slept the whole ride in."

"Figures," she answered with a huge smile.

Jeremy came up behind us with a bright orange shirt, matching knee high socks, and khaki shorts. His beady brown eyes smiled from behind his matching bright-orange rimmed glasses.

"Hey sunshine," I said, holding my arms out to him.

"Hey Emma," he said, pressing his glasses back on his face. "Looks like we came just in time. You look like you could use some sunshine."

"Come here, you," I said, wrapping him in a hug.

"I'm glad to see none of the wildlife has taken a bite out of you," he noted.

I laughed, and then started crying. I didn't plan on crying, it just happened. It was probably the fact that I finally saw their awesome faces. "You don't know how good it is to see you both."

"No tears, girl. We're here for the next four days. Happy faces. Only happy faces allowed during this trip," Lia scolded.

"You've got it," I said, wiping my tears.

They each put an arm around me and we headed down the escalator toward baggage claim.

Kade stayed a distance behind giving us our privacy.

"So, Emma, why the *hell* didn't you contact us for *four damn months?*" Jeremy questioned, walking toward the luggage carousel. "Lia thought you were dead. She wanted to call the Alaska State Troopers and the FBI."

"It's complicated, and I seriously don't think either of you would believe the stories if I told you," I huffed.

"Well, we're here for four whole days. That's ninety-six hours for you to spill," Jeremy noted.

Lia looked over my shoulder. Her eyes widened, and she squeezed my arm tightly. "Holy hell, Emma. Is that Kade?" she rasped.

"Ouch," I said flatly, trying to loosen her grip. "Yes, it is."

"Sorry! But, oh my God! He's even hotter than I remember. And, who is that mean looking guy next to him?"

"That would be Malachi. Don't stare. He hates when people stare at him, and will not hesitate to come over and hit you."

"Oh my God! Are you serious?" she whipped her head back to the front. Her hand flew up to her chest, and her eyes widened with fear.

I burst into laughter. "I'm just kidding, Lia. He's harmless, and just a family friend."

"Damn you, Emma," she said slapping me. "I almost freaking peed myself."

"Well, you better hold it," I said.

"Why?" She questioned.

"Because the bathrooms here are deadly."

Lia rolled her eyes at me. "Right. So what is there to do here? I've heard there are tons of things."

"Oh, I've been on quite the adventure since I've arrived."

Lia eyed me. "Did Kade take you on this adventure?"

"Parts of it," I smiled.

"Stop right now. I don't want to hear any of this," Jeremy said, glaring at us.

"I seriously missed you guys," I laughed, throwing my arms around their necks again.

"We were really worried about you," he admitted.

"There were a few bad things that did happen, but I'd rather not talk about any of that right now. Right now, I just want to spend some fun times, and make new, happy memories with my best friends."

"Sounds good to me," Lia chimed. "Sooo, does Kade have a brother? Like a twin? An identical, or slightly hotter twin?"

"Lia. Focus," Jeremy huffed.

"I am, Jeremy, can't you tell? Laser focus. Anyway, I'm on vacation and away from my parents. Let me be free."

"Oh God. You two are going to give me a heart attack."

"Whatever, Jeremy. Maybe Kade has a sister for you," she teased.

"Yeah, and with my luck, she's probably a slightly bigger, manlier version of Mr. Beefcake over there...No, I don't need any of that. I just want a vacation." He rolled his eyes and shook his head.

Lia giggled and turned her focus back to me. "So…does he have any brothers?" She was dead serious.

"Actually, he does have a few. They aren't blood brothers, but they are very close, and they are very handsome."

"Are they sexy handsome? Like Kade? I mean, have you seen his ass?" Her eyebrows wiggled.

I giggled, hoping Kade heard that last comment. "Yes. Very sexy," I confirmed

"Can we go now?" Jeremy sighed, collecting his luggage from the carousel. "Luggage, Lia. Focus. They won't think you're sexy when you're wearing the same clothes for four days."

"Oh, fine. It's the turquoise zebra print coming around," she said, pointing to her bag.

After we collected their luggage, we all headed back out to the parking garage.

"Whoa, check out that Hummer," Jeremy said, gawking.

"That's our ride," I chimed.

"No way. Are you serious?" He questioned. A smile widened on his face.

"Dead serious," I winked.

He exhaled hard, obviously impressed.

And that was a huge score.

As we neared the car, the doors unlocked. Malachi pulled open the rear passenger door, and I suddenly watched Lia freeze as she caught sight Dominic.

"Lia, are you okay?" I giggled.

She swallowed, and turned to me. "No wonder you didn't call me. You were holding out. Don't worry, I would have done the same," she said softly.

Little did she know, they could hear her every word.

Dominic smiled and Malachi shook his head and jumped in the front. Jeremy and Lia took the middle seat, and Kade and I cozily squished in the back.

"Nice ride," Jeremy noted.

"Yeah, it's alright. Gets us from A to Z," Dominic answered. "So you're both friends of Emma?"

"For the past three years," Jeremy said.

"And your names are?" Dominic asked.

I was glad he was making small talk. It would help kill some of the time.

"I'm Jeremy Needles and this is Lia Ling. We come from LA."

"Los Angeles. The city of the Angels," Dominic said, glancing at Malachi.

I didn't realize the truth until Dom said it. I'd lived in the city of the Angels, not having a clue I was part of that world.

Dominic kept asking questions about their upbringing, school, and other random things. I was glad because it kept Jeremy's mind busy. We were on a long, lonely highway headed back out to Delta Junction when Lia looked out the window.

"Wow, those are some huge birds. What are they? Ravens?"

I leaned over Kade and peeked out. "FALLEN!" I screamed.

"Fallen?" Lia turned back to me, her face twisted.

Dominic suddenly punched the gas. I glanced behind us and

noticed the second Hummer did the same. Malachi grabbed a walkie.

"Samuel, can you hear me?" he said.

"Yes, I'm here," he answered.

"Fallen at three o'clock."

"How many?"

"Four."

"Roger. You'll have to pull over someplace safe."

Lia twisted back to me. "Emma, what the hell is going on? What is a Fallen, and why are we speeding?" Her eyes narrowed. She and Jeremy focused their attention on me, waiting for an answer.

Suddenly the right side of the Hummer was hit hard. Dominic hit the brakes and we spun out. Lia screamed. Her eyes popped wide with horror as her tiny frame flew onto the floor. Jeremy grabbed the seat and held on, his eyes filled with terror.

"Emma. What the hell is going on?" Jeremy shrieked.

"Malachi!" I yelled. His head twisted back. "Sleeper!"

I didn't want to do this to my friends, but I knew they wouldn't understand or be able to handle this situation. It would be easier if they were asleep and not completely freaking out.

"I'm sorry. I didn't want any of this to happen," I said. My heart was completely crushed.

Malachi whispered into Jeremy's ear and he went limp. He then helped the badly shaken Lia off the floor. As soon as she saw Jeremy she began screaming uncontrollably.

"Lia, he's fine. It'll be okay. I promise." I tried to comfort her.

I suddenly felt sick to my stomach. The one thing I was praying wouldn't happen, did. And it started only a few hours after they arrived. How was I going to explain this? Their lives were in my hands.

As Malachi whispered into her ear I watched her eyes roll back and her body go limp.

"Emma. We need to get you out of here," Kade urged.

"We *all* need to get out of here," I corrected him.

Dominic pulled off onto a side road and into the trees. The second Hummer followed right behind. We all got out and pulled our weapons.

ELEVEN

S AMUEL CAME RUNNING TO OUR car. "Are you all okay?"

"Yes," I said, nodding to Lia and Jeremy. "We used the sleeper on my friends."

"Smart thinking. It's better this way," he confirmed.

"Emma, you stay here with your friends. Kade, Malachi, and Dominic, you stay with them. I'll take Ethon, Bane, and Azzah and catch them in the air."

"I thought your wings weren't ready yet?" I questioned.

"Don't worry. They'll be fine. It'll hurt a bit, but they are strong enough to carry me. It's nothing I can't handle," Samuel smiled. I knew he would say anything to make me feel better. He was doing this to save me.

Ethon glanced at me, and then at Kade, who was by my side. Both sets of eyes steeled on one another, each filled with hate.

A dark shadow passed above, causing a whirlwind around us.

Everyone agreed to their duty, and all four Fallen bore their beautiful black wings. Ethon glanced at me one last time, and shot off into the sky. There was a large clearing just ahead. I ran forward, wanting to witness the battle.

"Emma," Kade said, stopping me.

"I want to see. Please." I pleaded. This was something I didn't want to miss.

He nodded. "Then don't leave my side."

I grabbed his hand and we headed to the clearing. We watched as the four evil Fallen drew their swords, preparing to battle Samuel, Ethon, Bane, and Azzah.

Samuel's wings did look just as strong as the others.

Ethon glanced down, and winked at me, making my stomach twist. I really hoped none of them would be hurt.

This was an unbelievable sight. Fallen fighting Fallen to protect us.

Suddenly, Lucian's Fallen shot forward with loud battle cries.

Ethon was the first to meet them. He effortlessly somersaulted in the air over the first, and then spread his wings. Spinning, he chopped off its head, using his wing as the weapon. It was so fast, the Fallen's eyes were still wide open from shock as its head separated from the rest of its body, dropping to the earth in a sideways spiral.

Then, Ethon unsheathed his sword and spun in the opposite direction, lopping off the next Fallen's head. He had just killed *two* of them in a matter of seconds, and with minimal effort. It was clear he could have handled all four Fallen by himself.

Damn, he was good.

Kade didn't move, but I knew he was watching, and wishing he was able to fight. My heart ached for him, remembering how many times he saved my life in the heat of battle. I could only imagine the negative thoughts running through his mind. And it didn't help matters that my other suitor – for lack of a better word – was the one inflicting all the damage.

I pushed closer to him, until my side molded against his. He wrapped his arm around me and squeezed my shoulder.

Samuel clashed swords so hard with the third one, sparks showered down all around us. I gasped, and held my breath. I knew he was a warrior, but he'd been out of battle for a while. The thought of losing him after I'd just found him was unbearable.

The sheer power with which they connected sent shockwaves outward, shaking the ground and trees around us. The Fallen swung his sword at Samuel's neck, but he ducked and the blade missed his head by fractions of an inch.

I screamed, and immediately threw my hands over my mouth.

Samuel briefly took his eyes off of his enemy to make sure I was okay. But in that split second, the Fallen raised his blade to slay him. My eyes widened, but before I could scream…Ethon flew at a lightning speed, knocking the Fallen away from Samuel.

I watched in complete awe and horror as Ethon took on the fight. But the Fallen was no match for him. Ethon gripped his sword and spun, effortlessly beheading his enemy.

I exhaled, not even realizing I was still holding my breath. That was way too close. Samuel could have been killed, but Ethon saved him.

Samuel turned to Ethon and gave him a nod of appreciation.

Bane and Azzah surrounded the last Fallen. Even he knew he didn't have a chance, and defeat was written on his face. Dropping his sword, he put his hands up in surrender.

"I don't want to fight with you brothers," he pleaded.

But the goons were ruthless and offered no mercy. Bane grabbed his head, Azzah grabbed his legs, and they pulled, ripping him apart. His headless body fell from the sky. In minutes, the beheaded bodies caught fire, and burned to ash.

Samuel and Ethon flew higher and searched the skies for any signs of additional Fallen.

"I don't think it will be safe to drive," Samuel said. "They know where we are. Malachi, you and Dominic will drive the vehicles back. Azzah, you and Kade will accompany them. The rest of us will fly back. We need to get them back to the house as quickly as we can."

I knew Kade felt helpless. I took hold of his hand. "I'll see you at home," I assured him.

His eyes remained distressed, but he forced a sad grin and nodded once.

Extracting Jeremy and Lia from the vehicles, Malachi placed Lia in Ethon's arms, while Dominic laid Jeremy in Bane's.

"Come, Emma," Samuel said.

Ethon stepped forward. "Samuel if we get attacked, you know I can outfly any of the Fallen. I can guarantee Emma's safety."

Samuel paused, weighing his words. "Alright, but you will stay with us, unless anything happens."

"Yes, sir," Ethon responded, gently handing Lia over to Samuel.

As soon as Samuel turned around, Ethon took a quick glance in my direction and winked. I narrowed my eyes and shook my head. He'd gotten what he wanted.

Striding toward me, he held out his hand. "You'll be flying the not-so-friendly-skies with me once again."

I hesitated, knowing what happened when I touched him.

"I promise I won't bite, unless you're into that kind of thing." His eyes flickered with a devilish grin.

"Just no fancy spins. The last time I flew with you, I had vertigo for hours," I warned.

"Deal. No spins, unless I have to," he agreed, drawing a cross over his heart.

I took a step closer, and cautiously placed my hand in his. Nearly dropping at the instant current coursing through my body, Ethon wrapped his arm around me, steadying my body against his.

"I've got you," he whispered. His breath sent a shiver down my spine.

"Thanks," I breathed, still trying to fight the magnetic pull of the bond. I glanced over to where the Hummers were parked, but they were no longer there.

"Ready?" Samuel asked.

Ethon and Bane gave a nod, and with one single flap, Samuel was airborne. Bane followed.

"Are you ready?" Ethon asked, his fiery eyes steeled on mine.

I nodded.

Before I could take another breath, we shot into the sky.

"It's completely gratifying to have you back in my arms," he admitted.

I didn't respond. I couldn't.

"You don't have to answer. I know what you felt when you touched me. The bond allows us to share emotions."

It *did* feel good to have him close again, but I also knew the majority of those emotions were from the bond.

"I hope I get to meet your friends soon."

"Maybe," I said, glancing ahead, at the limp limbs of my sleeping friends. They would never forgive me if they found out. "But you're supposed to remain anonymous."

"True, but I think your Guardian is getting the preferential treatment. I know your friends would love me once they met me, and then they would join me in my campaign to win your heart."

"So you want to use them as pawns?" I questioned.

"No. Not pawns. They'd want to do it of their own free will," he admitted with a smile.

"Well, I'm sure they'd love to meet you, but I just wouldn't know how to introduce you. They've already met Kade, and my girlfriend is completely infatuated with him. In fact, she asked if he had a twin brother."

He huffed. "That's because she hasn't met me yet."

"Maybe. But you also have to remember they're human, and your red eyes *might* be a bit much. My girlfriend might have nightmares."

"Or, miraculous dreams," he whispered. For a moment I was captured by the swirling glow of his eyes. "Plus," he said, snapping me back to reality, "I've acquired those disposable plastics which alter eye color. They help me blend in the midst of mortals."

"You mean contacts?" I giggled.

"Yes. Contacts," he acknowledged.

"It looks like you've covered your bases. I'll figure out a way for you to meet them."

"Just tell them I'm the son of an old family friend. You wouldn't even be lying."

"That might work," I admitted. He was trying to fit in, and I guess I appreciated that, even if he had ulterior motives. He was ultimately trying to win my heart.

He smiled. "Of course it will work. And I promise to be on my best behavior."

"Why do I find that hard to believe?"

"Have I given you any reason to doubt me?"

I thought about it. "No."

"Then, why start now?" I looked into his eyes, trying to find anything which would contradict his words.

Kade warned me not to trust him but so far Ethon hadn't given me any reason not to. Deep inside though, I knew there was something. A very mysterious something about Ethon I couldn't put my finger on. He was the ultimate bad boy. The son of Lucifer. He had to have a flaw.

But outwardly, he was a far cry from the depictions given by mortal beings. I'd always assumed them to be horrifying, monstrous creatures - beasts with horns and pitchforks. Much to my surprise, it was to the contrary.

The Fallen were beautiful.

Even Bane and Azzah, behind their permanent scowls, outgrown beards, and hardened hearts, weren't unattractive. Cleaned up and clean-cut, I could see how they would be attractive.

"You don't ever have to be afraid of me. I may come from a dark and evil place, but that's not who I am. I'm not my father, and I have no intention of following in his footsteps."

I made the mistake of looking into his eyes a little too long, and was instantly bewitched, like a moth to flame.

"Shouldn't you be watching what's ahead of you?" I said, breathless.

"I have total peripheral vision, and sight comparable to a hawk. Besides, how could I look away from the perfection in my arms," he whispered.

"Ethon," I exhaled. My body was becoming weak, melting into his. Electricity buzzed around us.

"You do something to me, Emma. Everything aches when you're distant. I crave you… and right now, I'm going to kiss you."

"My father is right in front of us."

"I can lose them in seconds if I wanted to," he said.

"Don't give him a reason to hate you," I said.

His eyes narrowed and a grin formed on his porcelain face. "So, you *do* like me?"

"I-I never said I didn't," I stuttered. I felt vulnerable under the weight of his gaze.

His fingers gently caressed my back, and then he slowed our flight. Glancing up quickly, he checked his positioning between Samuel and Bane.

Slowly and carefully, his hand traveled up my spine and rested on the back of my neck. His eyes fixed back on mine and started to burn a bright reddish-orange. The alluring power of the bond was growing, becoming overwhelmingly intense. It was seductive, and inevitable...we were going to kiss.

The wind whipped around us, but all I felt was the warmth generated from our mutual passion. I was trapped by his magnetism.

I closed my eyes, but my body was fully aware of what was happening. Heart racing, my breath was quick and ragged. A pulse of energy surged through my body as his lips softly pressed against mine, his fingers threading through my hair. A moan escaped my lips as his velvety tongue found entrance.

A sudden euphoria blanketed us. Flying made it even more exhilarating.

The bond was magical, and at this moment, I could feel his emotions - how much he wanted to love and protect me.

The bond with Ethon was so raw and intense.

Bam!

We were suddenly struck from the side and our lips unlocked. I screamed as I almost fell from his grip, feeling the weightless drop in my stomach. Ethon captured me, pulling me closer and tried to regain his balance.

His eyes snapped up and burned with a dark, fiery flame. Rage.

Bane had hit us. His face was hard and his eyes had gone completely black. I knew he was disapproving. He snarled, making a head gesture to let us know he had seen, and if we kept it up, Samuel would too.

"Emma, are you alright?" Samuel asked, quickly glancing back.

"Yes," I answered. "We almost hit a bird." I had to think of something quick, and that was the most logical thing I could think of.

"Be careful with my daughter, Ethon," he said.

"If anything tries to harm her, I will kill it," Ethon answered flatly, his eyes still locked onto Bane. His breath and heartbeat had increased. I also heard *and felt* a deep growl rumbling from within. It scared me. He looked like he would rip Bane apart.

I gently placed my hand on the side of his face, and as I did, his focus turned back to me. As soon as his eyes fixed on mine, they slowly returned to their normal, more subdued color.

"It's okay," I whispered.

"If I dropped you, I would have killed him." His face became hard again, and the edges of his eyes flickered with the dark red flame.

"Ethon, he's just looking out for you, per his orders. If my father saw us, believe me, it could have been much worse than just a bump."

His brow furrowed. Taking in a deep breath, he exhaled. The flames in his eyes slowly diminished. "I thought you didn't care for my goons," he finally said.

I gasped. "What? How did you?" I didn't remember mentioning, to anyone, that I referred to his companions as *goons*. I swear I only used that term in my mind.

Ethon looked amused. "You didn't think I'd give away all my secrets, did you?"

"Secrets? What secrets?" I narrowed my eyes.

"Every secret embedded in me will be unlocked and revealed *only if you choose me.*"

"Oh. So you're using bribery now?" I challenged.

"If it helps…then yes," he said flatly.

"You may have tricks up your sleeve, but I still hold the key."

"Oh, Emma," Ethon breathed. "You have no idea of the trickery I possess." His eyes smile widened.

I'd like to find out.

Ethon suddenly laughed, he leaned in, tickling my ear as he whispered, "Are you sure? Because I'd be more willing to show you."

I covered my mouth with my hand, looking into his mischievous eyes.

Was he reading my mind? Was that even possible? If he could, that would be rude. Reading minds was a total invasion of privacy. I treasured my private thoughts, and random conversations with myself. Having someone else swimming around in my mind…well, that was totally not cool.

"You can read my mind, can't you?" I questioned. I figured I'd come straight out and ask, instead of wondering.

His eyes showed no emotion, and gave me nothing. He grinned at me and shrugged.

"You're evil," I huffed.

"Inherently."

Dammit. Now I'd have to keep my mind blank around him. However…if he could read minds, he would already know what I was planning.

Good Lord. This completely sucked.

Blank. White. Nothingness. I needed to clear my mind.

How do monks do this? Okay, come on Emma. We've got this.

I closed my eyes, and thought of white clouds floating in the sky.

"What are you doing?" Ethon laughed.

"Focusing," I answered.

"On what?"

"Keeping you out of my mind." I opened one eye to peek at him, and saw him shaking his head. A smile was plastered on his face. "What?"

"In time you'll see," he said.

"See what?"

"That you'll choose me."

"You don't know that, and besides, my time is very fragile these days. I may not even make it to my transformation."

"Like I said before, you don't have to worry about Lucian while I'm around. He will die by my hand if he tries to hurt you. That is a promise."

"Thank you," I said.

"For what?"

"For wanting to protect me."

"It's an unwilled impulse," he answered.

I hugged him. "Well, thank you anyway."

He pressed his lips to my cheek, and then focused forward. "Let's get you home safely."

TWELVE

WE ENCOUNTERED NO ADDITIONAL PROBLEMS the rest of the flight home. It was serene. The darkening sky was the most beautiful blue, and the puffs of cirrocumulus clouds were painted in a sorbet of pink, orange, and lavender.

Ethon never loosened his grip around me, and I felt comfortable in his arms, gliding just above the tree lines.

When I glanced down, everything was a blur and I became dizzy, so I kept most of my focus on either the sky above, or Ethon. A few times during flight, he'd leaned down and pressed his lips to my forehead.

For a devil boy, he seemed to be quite the gentleman, and I wondered where he'd picked up those traits. On the other hand, I'd caught a glimpse of fire in his eyes, and had seen the potential for what he could do. There weren't many who could match him.

He was very complicated, and yet, intriguing. When I directed my gaze to his face, I'd hoped to read his expressions - see what he was thinking. But he was like a closed book, only offering a pretty cover.

Snap out of it, Emma.

There were more important things to worry about right now. I had to come up with some kind of story to tell Jeremy and Lia. When they woke up, they would have so many questions.

I knew Lia would be pissed. I glanced at their limp bodies being carried by Samuel and Bane. At least they were peaceful at the moment.

When we arrived at the house, Alaine panicked at first, but then focused on getting them settled on beds in their own rooms. Lia was in the room next to me, and Jeremy was a floor down, on the opposite side, in a room next to Kade. I left a note on their nightstands to come to my room when they woke up. It would be the one with a pink ribbon tied to the doorknob.

I knew it would be a few more hours before they woke, so I took a shower and readied myself for the onslaught of questions. I was a little apprehensive about trying to explain things to Jeremy. I didn't know if he'd believe anything.

I needed help. Maybe I could bring Courtney and Caleb into the mix. The more I thought about it, the more it seemed like a great plan. They were normal humans like Jeremy and Lia, and I had a feeling they would get along really well.

I exited my room and knocked on Courtney's door. In a few

seconds, it swung open.

"Emma!" she smiled, sticking her head out looking down the hall. "I thought your friends were here?"

"They are," I dragged, "but we ran into some Fallen on our way here."

"Oh my God. Are they alright?" She gasped, throwing her hand over her mouth.

"Yes, they're fine. They're actually sleeping."

"Both of them? Sleeping? After being attacked?" He eyes widened even more.

"Yes, they were freaking out, so we had to use the sleeper on them." I explained.

"Oh my goodness. Caleb told me about the sleeper," her eyes furrowed. "Okay, so what do you want me to do?"

"I just need you and Caleb to hang out with us tonight. The thing is…my friends can't find out about the Angels or Fallen. They can't know about any of it. As far as they are concerned, we're all normal humans. So, I need your help to keep them busy, and to hopefully divert their attention when they begin asking too many questions."

"I can definitely do that. Do you want me to get Caleb?" She questioned.

"Yes, please. Just meet me in my room, and bring your board games."

"You got it." Giving a thumbs-up, she then bounded down the hall toward Caleb's room.

I wondered when Kade and the others would return. Probably soon.

Ethon and Bane were already in the tower, and Samuel had returned to the cottage after talking to Alaine.

I went back into my room and waited. About ten minutes later, there was a knock at the door. When I opened it, Caleb and Courtney were standing with their arms filled with board games and snacks.

I gave Caleb a quick rundown of the situation, and he was completely onboard. They were thrilled to be a part of a secret mission, and were also excited to meet my best friends from LA. To pass the time, the three of us ended up sitting on the floor, playing cards. We were right in the middle of our fifth game when we heard a soft knock at the door.

"Emma?"

"Come in," I yelled.

The knob twisted, and Lia peeked inside. Her eyes were swollen with sleep and she looked completely confused.

"Come in, Lia!"

She opened the door and walked in. Her normally stick-straight, black hair was sticking up on one side, and her glasses were a bit crooked.

"How did we get here? What happened?" she asked, her almond shaped eyes were barely slits as she squinted behind her glasses.

"In the Hummer. You and Jeremy knocked out. You must have been exhausted from flying."

"I guess," she said. I knew she was completely boggled. She looked over to Courtney and Caleb and didn't say anything else.

I jumped up and ran to her, and threw my arms around her. "Lia, I want you to meet my sort-of-siblings, Courtney and Caleb.

They were adopted by Alaine when they were younger." I led her toward them.

"Hi," she said, pushing a polite smile.

"Hi," they echoed.

"Emma, seriously, what the hell happened? All I remember was being surrounded by hot guys, well…mostly hot guys. No offense to Jeremy. Then, I remembered these huge black birds outside the car window…before everything went blank. The next thing I know, I'm waking up in an unfamiliar room, on an unfamiliar bed. I thought I was in some kind of crazy nightmare, until I saw your note."

"You just knocked out. I'm not sure what else to tell you. One minute you were talking, and the next you were sleeping. You must have been exhausted. Did you even get any sleep before you came here?"

"No. We stayed up the whole night because we were too excited. But that was so strange. I hope we weren't exposed to carbon monoxide poisoning. I've heard of people knocking out, and it could be deadly."

"I don't know, but at least you're fine now," I noted. "You are fine, right?"

"Yes, just still a little tired," she said.

"Emma?" Jeremy said, entering behind us yawning.

"Hey, Jeremy!" I said, heading up to him.

"What happened?"

"I don't know. You both just completely knocked out."

"How in the heck could we both fall asleep, at the exact same time?" Jeremy questioned.

"Were you up late?"

"Well, we didn't sleep. We stayed up all night eating candy and drinking soda," Lia said.

"Then that's it," Caleb jumped in. "You both had a sugar crash. It happens if you eat too much sugar. But combine it with lack of sleep and...*bam*! You're out cold."

"I guess that's possible," Jeremy agreed, with another yawn.

Phew. Maybe the fifth degree would end soon.

Caleb and Courtney really hit it off with Jeremy and Lia, so much in fact, I felt like – and was – a fifth wheel.

Lia and Caleb flirted with each other all night, and Jeremy and Courtney even hit it off. They weren't flirting, but Courtney kept him busy with her many questions about LA. Jeremy was more than happy to give his detailed answers.

It was great to have help, and I started to believe we could actually pull this off. I really wanted them to have fun. Courtney and Caleb were my lifesavers.

It was nearly 2am when everyone said goodnight, and walked back to their rooms. I turned off my light and snuggled into bed, exhausted. It had been a long day, full of stress.

Exhaling loud and long, I closed my eyes, hoping to fall into darkness.

I awoke suddenly in a cold, dark room. A spotlight landed on a figure standing about a hundred feet in front of me. It was a boy with his back to me, and he was shirtless. His arms were listless and dropped to his sides. His head was facing downward.

"Hello?" I called softly. There was no answer. He didn't even move.

As I walked closer, I noticed his hands were balled into tight fists, and his back was badly scarred and covered in blood.

My heart began to race, and I could hear the sound of my breath quicken.

I stepped even closer to the figure, and quickly covered my mouth to try and keep down the rising vomit.

Two gaping holes oozed slowly, but heavily, from either side of his shoulder blades. I could see bone peeking from beneath the open flesh. White feathers, stained with crimson, were strewn about the floor. Some were caught within the thick blood.

It looked as if he once had wings, but they had been ripped from his back.

"Can I help you?" I breathed, reaching out to his arm. When I touched it, his head whipped sideways.

No!

"Kade! What the hell happened?" I cried frantically. I reached out to grab his arm, and as soon as I touched him, his skin felt ice cold and he was unresponsive. His eyes glazed over, looking bewildered.

"How did you get here? Kade, we need to get out of here!" I yelled, tugging his arm. "Kade!"

Why would he be in this dark place? And why did he have gaping holes in his back? He was a Guardian, and Guardians didn't have wings.

His body suddenly fell limp into my arms, and I dropped under his weight. I used every bit of strength I had to turn him on his side, and then carefully rested his head in my lap. I brushed dampened hair from his forehead.

"Kade. Please answer me. What happened? Why are you here? Where are we?" There was still no response, and his eyes remained closed. *"Please, baby. Open your eyes. I need you,"* I sobbed, pleading. *I felt completely lost. Holding him in my arms, there was nothing I could do to help him.*

Kade's eyes flickered and slowly opened. The once hazel eyes I'd become familiar with had been tainted. Bright red veins snaked throughout them, making him look almost alien.

"For you," he whispered. *"I did it for you."*

"What? What did you do for me?"

His arm lifted and his weak fingers traced the side of my face, and then dropped, limp. His eyes went blank, and the corners started to change color. Slowly creeping inward, a white fog covered his eyes, until they were icy, dead white.

"Kade!" I screamed. *"Kade!"* I shook him, but he didn't move or respond.

"No. You can't die. You can't leave me. Please. Come back," I sobbed, rocking his limp body in my arms.

A boisterous, wicked laugh echoed through the cavernous room. I looked around, but could only see pitch black. The evil laughter made my skin crawl. I turned and looked behind me, and there, burning in the darkness were two bright crimson eyes.

"I hate you!" I screamed. *"I hate you!"*

I shot up, my breath hitched in my throat. Sweat trickled down my brow, and my face was soaked with tears. I glanced at the clock. 3:17am.

"Kade," I whispered.

I had to see him. I had to make sure he was okay.

THIRTEEN

I PUSHED THE BLANKETS OFF me, and jumped out of bed. I made my way to the door, quietly opening and then shutting it behind me. The hallway was eerily dark and quiet, but I continued, attempting to be soundless. My pulse was still racing, and I still had the lingering ache in my chest seeing Kade's dead body in my arms.

I went down the flight of stairs and made my way to his door.

I knew if I knocked, I'd wake everyone up, so I decided to just enter. I hoped he wouldn't think I was an intruder, and attack me.

I sucked in a deep breath and slowly turned the knob.

The latch was unlocked, so I opened it. The hinges squeaked a bit, but the room inside was dark. I pushed in.

"Kade?" I whispered. I hoped he would hear me. "Kade?"

A light clicked on.

"Emma?" Kade sat up shirtless, his hair in its perfect disheveled form.

"Yes. It's me. I'm sorry. I – I just had a bad dream, and I had to see you." When I heard myself say the words, I realized I sounded like an idiot.

He jumped out of bed and walked over to me, stopping inches away. His sweet, spicy scent filled the space around me, making me dizzy. He lifted his arm and quietly snapped the door shut.

"Come here," he said, wrapping me in the warmth of his arms. "Is everything okay?"

"It is now," I breathed into his chest, hugging him back. My heart was still trying to settle, after realizing he was here and alive.

He led me over to the bed and we sat. "Do you want to tell me what happened?"

I paused. The nightmare was evil and horrifying, and I certainly didn't want to give him the details or relive them.

"I just - I thought I'd lost you," I whispered. "And, I felt so lost and alone."

His beautiful eyes twinkled as they looked at me, and then he smiled, making my heart patter.

"So you came to make sure I was still alive?" His eyes studied mine.

"Yes. You didn't let me know you made it home safely. I was really worried."

"Don't worry. I'm not going anywhere," he promised.

"Good. Because I need you. You're the only one who seems to hold me together, and you are *my* Guardian."

"I am," he breathed, leaning over and lightly kissing my nose. "So what now?"

I leaned back and yawned, still exhausted. I'd only slept for an hour, and I knew I'd have a crazy day with Jeremy and Lia in the morning.

"You must be exhausted," he noted.

"Very," I answered, my eyes were now watering.

"Would you like me to walk you back to your room?"

"No," I answered. His eyes narrowed. "Could I stay here with you for a while?"

"If that's what you want. Of course," he said.

"I just need to have you close right now."

He leaned forward and cradled my face in his fingers. "Is this close enough?" He pressed his warm lips to mine.

"Mmmhmm," I hummed into his mouth.

He smiled and then pulled back. "We can't get too carried away. This could get out of hand way too fast," he said with a smirk on his face.

"It could," I agreed. I scooted back to the middle of the bed and sat crisscrossed. "Hey, can I ask you something?"

"Anything," he answered, lying down next to me.

"I know you were a Guardian, you came from Midway, and that they assigned you to be my Guardian. But aside from that, I don't know much of anything about your past. I want to know more. I want to know about your parents, and about your childhood."

He smiled and shook his head.

"I'm sorry. I don't mean to pry."

"No. It's not that," he said, turning to me. "It's just that no one has ever asked me that before."

"No one?"

"No."

"Well, I'd really like to know about the first boy to steal my heart," I smiled. His face brightened as his eyes fastened on mine. My insides felt like they'd melted into a puddle of warm mush. He found my hands, and I laced my fingers through his, joining us together.

He turned, lying prostrate on his back; his eyes, searching for his past.

I waited patiently, anticipating his story. I was finally going to learn about this magical, angel boy who was dropped into my life.

"Well," he started. "I was born one hundred and seventy-nine years ago." He turned and glanced at me.

Okay, maybe he wasn't a boy. "One hundred and seventy-nine?" I swallowed. "I think you should know...at that age, on earth, you'd be known as a cradle robber," I giggled.

"If I were that age in mortal years, I'd be buried six feet under," he noted.

"Good point. So, in immortal years, you're how old?" I asked.

"Let's just say nineteen. I think two years your senior would work," he nodded.

"Well you do look about nineteen."

"Then we'll stick to nineteen, and now that I'm mortal, we can go from there."

"Do you have a birth day?"

"In the Otherworld we don't keep track of the day, but every mortal year we are presented with a gold coin. Once one has collected five hundred coins, they get their wings; unless they earn them, and earning them is almost impossible to do. I have one hundred and seventy-nine of them."

"You only had 321 years left," I smiled. "So where did you live?"

"I grew up in a place called Meadow of Songs. My mother and father still reside there. The summers in Alaska remind me of home. It's the most beautiful place, but there are no seasons. The grass, the trees, they are greenest green you could ever imagine. The sky is the purest blue. There is nothing imperfect in the realms. You could pick any fruit from a tree, and it would always be ripe and sweet. There is no shortage, and there is no evil."

"So you lived in Heaven?"

"Yes, mortals call it Heaven. We call it Grandia, or the Great Beyond."

His eyes suddenly swirled with memories.

"Tell me about your parents."

The corner of his lips curled upward and his eyes became distant. "My mother, well, she is radiant. Beautiful. Her eyes are deep amber, with flecks of gold. When she smiles, it radiates like a halo around her. Her voice is magical and sweeter than honey. She's a Worshiper."

"A Worshiper?" I questioned.

He nodded. "Worshipers fill Grandia with beautiful music. When a Worshiper opens their mouth, beautiful melodies spring forth and float through the air like an enchanted medicine, touching and filling everyone around them with tranquility and happiness. I was charmed as a child, having her transcendental lullaby's lay me to sleep each night."

"It must have been magical."

"It was. She would love you," he said, turning to me.

"What's her name?"

"Arella."

"Arella," I breathed. "That's such a beautiful name. And, what about your father?"

"My father is everything I ever want to become. If Angels could, they would envy him. Where ever he is, there is laughter. Whenever you meet him, you feel as if you've known him forever. He is filled with truth and guidance, but he is also very gentle. His presence and touch bring healing. His constant missions kept him from home, but my mother and I never doubted his love."

"What's his name?"

"Raphael."

"Why does his name sound so familiar? I've heard it before, from one of the few times we attended church."

"You probably have. He is an Archangel."

"An Archangel?"

"Archangels are the highest ranking Angels, chosen by the creator himself. Michael was the very first."

"Michael? The one who's dagger I have?" I gasped.

"Yes. He's the leader of all the Archangels."

"Wow, this world never ceases to amaze me. Your parents seem like the most amazing immortal beings. Now I know why you are so perfect. You were given the best of them."

"I'm far from perfect," he said.

"Not to me," I answered. "I hope I'll get to meet them one day."

"Maybe you will," he said. "And if you do, give them my love."

"Why? You'll have to introduce me."

"Not as a mortal," he said sadly.

"You mean you can't ever see them again?"

"Not in this form."

"Oh my God. Kade..." I exhaled. My stomach twisted.

"Don't be sorry, Emma. Things will work out in the end. You'll see. And my parents, they know why I chose this path."

"They must hate me for it." I couldn't imagine them ever loving me, knowing what he gave up for me.

"Never. My parents could never hate, especially you," he said, rising to his elbow. "I know they are proud of the decision I made."

"Which decision?" I whispered.

"You," he answered.

I tried to hold back the tears, but I couldn't.

"I think that's enough for tonight. You should get some sleep. You have guests to entertain and they'll be awake in a few hours."

I nodded and curled up next to him. He tucked me under the warmth of his blanket, and held me in his arms.

I knew one thing was certain. I could give my whole heart to Kade, and trust him with my life. His love and devotion had already been proven unwavering. The only downfall would be watching his mortal body age, or get sick and diseased, and eventually die.

One way or another, I would lose him. It would be much sooner than I'd ever want to, and the thought of that possibility, made my heart ache all over again. I didn't think I could bear losing someone who had my heart.

He held me tightly. My body melted and molded into his side, his warmth soothed me. In his arms, I felt whole and complete. It was hard to explain, yet, so simple for my heart to understand.

"Don't give up on me, Emma," he whispered, so quietly I almost didn't hear.

"Never," I answered.

The soft thrumming of his pulse and steadiness of his breath, slowly lulled me to sleep.

⟨⟨⟩⟩

The next morning I woke to sounds of laughter in the hall. I shot up and gasped.

Kade.

I turned, but he wasn't there. As I glanced around, I quickly realized I was back in my own room, tucked in my own bed.

How the heck did I get here? Was I with him, or was it all just a dream?

I raised my arm to my nose and inhaled. A smile automatically formed on my lips as I caught his lingering scent.

It had been real.

FOURTEEN

I QUICKLY JUMPED OUT OF bed and headed for the bathroom. I knew Lia and Jeremy would be up soon, especially with the racket going on outside. Knowing them, they were probably part of it. I quickly groomed myself and changed into some jeans and a long sleeved lavender t-shirt. I also grabbed a matching lavender hoodie, and as soon as I threw it over my head, there was a knock at the door.

"Come in," I called.

The door opened and Lia and Jeremy stood there.

"What are you doing out there? Get your behinds in here," I said running up and throwing my arms around them. "So what's the plan? Did you guys want to do something today?"

"Duh. We didn't only come here to make sure your sorry butt was alive. We came for adventure," Jeremy said.

"Adventure? You and adventure don't really go together," I said, with a raised brow. Jeremy was not the adventurous type. His adventure lied in slaying enemies from behind a controller or the pages of his books.

"Yes, that is true, but I'm living large in Alaska," he winked.

"Whatever, Jeremy," Lia huffed. "The only thing living large is your brain."

"I'll admit. My head is a bit larger than the normal human being, but that's only because there's too much awesome in it. My brain just needs a large container," he said. Lia and I looked at each other started laughing.

"Jeremy, you are awesome," I admitted.

He nodded with a smirk.

"Okay. So, Caleb was telling us about this lake not too far from here. He said it's private and about a mile away. It has a swinging rope, a few boats, and a volleyball net," Jeremy said.

"Yes! Doesn't that sound like fun, Emma?" Lia chimed.

NO! Damn it, Caleb. He was supposed to be helping me keep them within the barrier. How the hell was I supposed to keep them safe a mile outside? We would have to gather everyone together on this one.

"Emma? If you don't want to go, just tell us," Jeremy said.

I didn't realize I'd frozen, running every horrible scenario imaginable through my mind.

"No, it's not that. I mean, it sounds great. Let me talk to Alaine and see if she can get us a ride."

"Hey Emma. Do you think that same guy who drove us in, can

drive us again?" Lia asked.

"Dominic?" I asked.

"Yes!" She squealed.

"I'm sure he'd love to come," I answered. "You two go get ready, and I'll go see if I can make the transportation arrangements. I'll meet you in the dining room for breakfast." I started heading out the door.

"Wait, where's the dining room?" Lia asked, just as Courtney walked by.

I grabbed Courtney. "She'll show you. Right, Court?"

"Of course. Just yell when you're ready. I'll leave my door open," she said.

"See you soon," I said.

"See ya." They both headed out toward their rooms, while I rushed down the stairs. Dominic and Malachi had just walked in from the kitchen.

"Hey, Emma," Dominic yelled.

"Hey, Dom. I was just going to come and look for you," I smiled widely.

"You were?" he asked.

"Yes. I need your Guardian services today. Caleb made the suggestion to go to some lake a mile away, and my friends really want to go."

"Dumb ass," Malachi huffed. "I was going to take a nap today."

"Sorry," I apologized.

"A nap? Well, I guess you *would* need one. You are getting old," Dominic snickered, slapping Malachi on the shoulder. He then gave me a secret wink.

"Screw you," Malachi retorted.

"Hell, I'm in. I've gotta school everyone on how to properly quadruple flip off the rope."

"Quadruple flip?" I gasped, throwing my hand on my chest, over exaggerating.

"Hell yeah. And you better make sure Kade's not watching when it happens. He gets a little jealous."

"Of you?" Malachi laughed.

"Dude, when these mortal chicks see what's under these garments ... it will be a swoon fest," he bragged.

"Don't you mean swine fest?" Malachi glared at him.

"Come on, Mal. Don't hate the player, hate the game. Not everyone was blessed with a complete package. At least you were given some cool fighting skills."

"Keep talking, Dom, or the only thing the girls will notice is your swollen jaw."

"He's attempting to be scary, Em. Don't laugh. It'll only make him angrier," Dom whispered.

Malachi suddenly swung his fist, but Dom ducked just in time.

"Dude, you need to work on your temper. Maybe you should go take a nap," Dominic badgered. I shook my head as he sprinted up the stairs.

"Dom. Will you drive us?" I yelled up after him.

"Anything for you," he answered. "I'll let Kade know."

"Thank you, I owe you one."

"Emma, you realize that everyone will need to coordinate this.

It's not just a simple trip to the lake. We will all have to be on full guard," Malachi said.

"I do. I was originally hoping we could all just stay in and watch movies, but Caleb opened his big mouth. I'm going to talk to Alaine right now. Do you think Thomas and Alexander would go too?"

"I think they'll be more than happy to get out of the cabin. I'll have them show up a little later, so it doesn't look like we're together. They can do their own thing on the other side of the lake."

"Sounds great. Thanks, Malachi."

"Yeah," he said in a nice voice, and then walked away.

I walked down the hall toward Alaine's study and knocked.

"Come in."

I stepped inside. She was sitting at her desk, reading a medical book.

"Good morning. I hope I'm not interrupting."

"No, of course not," she said, placing the book face down. "Good morning, sweetheart. Did everyone sleep well?"

"Yes, but we have a bit of a problem." I scrunched my face.

She exhaled. "Does this involve leaving the barrier?"

"It does. Caleb suggested they go to some lake a mile from here. He mentioned a rope swing and boats, and they got excited. They really want to go."

Rolling her eyes, she said, "I'll need to talk to, Caleb. I know of the lake. It's part of my property, and it is a mile away. Have you talked to the guys?"

"I talked to Dominic and Malachi. They both said they'll be coming. Malachi is going to ask Thomas and Alexander to meet us there, so it doesn't look like we're together. I know Kade will come."

"Alright, I'll talk to Samuel and get cooperation from Ethon and his company. We'll need their help. Did you happen to see James out there?" she asked.

"No, sorry. I haven't seen James in a few days."

"He's been pretty elusive. He thinks he should be undercover as well," she laughed. "Don't worry. I'll handle it. What time were you thinking of going?"

"After breakfast?" I was unsure if that was enough time.

"I'll gather the guys. Go ahead and take your friends to eat, and we'll all meet downstairs in let's say, two hours?"

"That sounds good to me, and I'm so sorry." I said.

"Don't be sorry. I had a feeling we wouldn't be able to keep them cooped up all four days. We have the best Guardians out there, and along with Samuel and the other Fallen, I think we'll be okay. If anything does happen, we have enough wings to get you and your friends to safety."

"Thank you." I turned to walk out.

"Emma," Alaine called.

"Yes?"

"Relax and have fun. There won't be many times like these, so make it count."

"I will," I smiled, and left.

Relax. I stopped in the hall, closed my eyes, took in a deep breath and exhaled, letting the stress melt away. I let my shoulders drop. I took in another deep breath and...

"There you are," Jeremy yelled, making me jump.

"Jeremy!" I scolded.

"What were you doing?" he asked, his face all scrunched up.

"I was trying to relax, until I was rudely interrupted."

"Well, just for future information, a hallway is not the best place to relax. People walk through hallways. You could be bumped, or someone might accidentally say 'hi' to you. The horror."

"Thanks, Jeremy. I'll be sure to remember that."

"Good. Now which way is the kitchen?"

"I thought Courtney was going to take you? And, where's Lia?"

"They left me. I guess I took too long, and Lia said she was *starving*. She obviously hasn't been to a third-world country," he stated, pushing his bright-orange glasses back on his pointed nose.

"Obviously not," I echoed. "Follow me, Einstein."

I led him down the hallway. "Your aunt must be super rich. This place is amazing. Is she a millionaire?"

"I don't know," I answered. "I think her late husband left her with a pretty big inheritance."

"Lucky. Maybe this will be yours one day," he said.

"Maybe," I answered. I'd never really given any thought to it, but then again, Alaine was immortal. This house would age long before she would.

The wonderful aromas of breakfast hit our noses as we turned and entered the hall to the kitchen.

"No way. Do I smell bacon?" Jeremy's face lit up.

"It smells like it. Looks like you've hit the jackpot, huh, Jeremy?"

"Hell yeah. You know me and bacon."

"I do," I smiled.

Bacon was his weakness. He could eat it for breakfast, lunch and dinner. My mom would make him bacon every time he and Lia slept over. She made his extra crispy, just how he liked it.

A smile formed on my lips at the memory.

"Good morning!" we heard as we walked into the kitchen.

"Good morning, Miss Lily," I answered.

"And who is this handsome gentleman with you?" she asked.

I watched Jeremy blush. "This is Jeremy. He's one of my best friends from Los Angeles."

"Well, it's great to meet you, Jeremy. I just met Lia a bit ago. She and Courtney are in the dining room."

"So what do we have for breakfast?" I asked.

"Oh honey, we have bacon, eggs, breakfast potatoes, and chocolate chip pancakes."

"My favorite," I said.

"Well, grab a plate. I set up buffet style today," she said pointing to the counter.

"Wow," Jeremy breathed.

All the food was kept warm in chaffing dishes. When Jeremy lifted the first lid, it was filled with extra crispy bacon.

"Praise the Lord! I can hear the Angels singing," he exhaled.

Miss Lilly and I laughed at his inadvertently witty remark.

"He's in heaven right now," I giggled.

"Well that's good. At least one of us is," she winked. "Take as much as you can eat."

Jeremy didn't hold back. He put about ten pieces of bacon on his plate, plus eggs, and two pancakes.

"Looks like you were pretty hungry too," I grinned.

"I guess," he said, crunching on a strip of bacon.

When we entered the room, Caleb, Courtney, and Lia were already seated and eating. Caleb looked up and I glared at him. He shrugged and lowered his head.

Jerkface. Today had better be safe, or he'd be in for it.

We took our seats opposite them. None of the guys were here so I assumed Alaine was briefing them.

"Hey guys," Lia waved. "This food is to die for. Jeremy, looks like you found the bacon."

"Oink, oink," he snorted.

Courtney burst out into laughter. We all looked at her.

"What? It was funny," she giggled.

"Girl, we need to get you out more often," Lia said. "Believe me, there are tons of funny people out there. Jeremy isn't one of them."

Courtney broke into laughter again.

"Is there something in that juice? If there is, hand it over," I said. "So, Caleb, I heard it was your big, bright idea to go to the lake." I steeled my eyes on him.

"Yes, the lake is awesome. I know your friends will love it." He kept his head down.

"Well, I hope everyone stays safe," I said.

"I'm sure they will."

"Hey Emma, is that cute guy gonna drive us?" Lia whispered across the table.

"He is," I winked at her.

"O-M-G!" she clapped.

"Who is she talking about?" Courtney asked.

"Probably Dominic. I doubt she'd be clapping for Malachi," Caleb huffed.

"Yes, that's his name. Dominic. He's so hot. Emma, you can have Kade, as long as I get Dominic."

"Lia, are you listening to yourself? The dude could probably get any chick he wanted, why would he want you?" Jeremy questioned.

"Hello, Jeremy. Because I'm the shizznit," she stood up and flicked her hair.

We all laughed. Lia was little, but she had a big personality and was actually really hilarious. Especially when she was comfortable with the people she was around.

"What nationality are you, Lia?" Caleb asked.

Lia glanced at him. Her eyes flirted, "Chinese."

"That's awesome. Have you ever been to China?"

"I have. Once. I even walked the Great Wall."

"You did?" Courtney blurted. "Isn't that the huge wall in Mulan?"

"Courtney," Caleb scolded. "Mulan is a cartoon."

"I know, but it still showed the Great Wall."

"Yes, it was the same wall in Mulan," Lia answered. "I like that movie."

"So do I," Courtney answered, giving Caleb the stink-eye.

After a lot of playful banter, laughing, and stuffing ourselves, we headed back upstairs.

"Okay, grab your things and we'll all meet in my room in a half-hour."

The four of them bounded up the stairs ahead of me. They looked like they were all getting along just fine, and that made me happy.

As they separated at the top of the stairs and went to their rooms, I noticed Kade's door open. My heart started to pitter-patter as I made my way up...then I missed a step and fell down.

"Dang it," I yelled, as I came down hard on my knee. It split open and there was blood seeping from a gash.

Before I could pull myself up, Kade was standing next to me.

I gasped. "How did you get here so fast?"

"I may be mortal, but that doesn't mean I don't have immortal qualities."

"I know. I've seen you in action."

"And?" He came so close, I could feel his warmth. Pulling off his shirt, he tore a piece off and gently wrapped it around my knee.

"You never fail to take my breath away," I sighed.

"That's good to know."

"You know, you didn't have to rip your shirt. There are bandages in the bathroom."

"I thought you'd appreciate the gesture."

"Oh, believe me. The gesture is *greatly* appreciated," Grinning, I appraised his perfectly sculpted six-pack.

We both laughed.

"What are you two lovebirds doing on the stairs? And Kade, why the hell do you keep losing your shirt around, Emma?" Dominic teased.

"I fell and he rescued me," I said. "His shirt is wrapped around my knee."

"Ahhhh....chivalry. It's not dead then," Dom said.

"No, it's not," I grinned.

"You better get your swimsuit on. We're leaving soon," Dominic said.

"There's no way I'm going swimming in the lake now. Not with a bloody knee. There are fish in it."

"Emma. They're fish, not sharks. *We eat them.* Besides, you'll probably be healed by the time we get there."

"Well they could be flesh-eating fish, like piranha or barracuda. You never know," I said.

"It's landlocked," Kade said softly. "It was dredged, but continually fed from an underground spring. There are some trout, but no barracuda or piranha."

"I think I'll stick to dry land. If you're real lucky, I may even get adventurous and go out in one of the boats."

"Suit yourself," Dom said. "I'll definitely be losing my shirt at the lake."

"Oh, I can't wait," I teased.

"Oh, Emma. You know you want me. Just admit it, and let's end this charade," he said, as he flexed his arms and popped his pecs.

"I want you, Dom," Kade muttered, "to get the hell out of here."

"Whatever. I'm going to get the Hummer. You both love me, and you know it."

Dominic bounced down the stairs and out the door. Kade helped me up, and wrapped his arm around my waist.

"You don't have to help me. I can walk the rest of the way just fine."

"I know, but I'm milking the chivalry card," he grinned. Out of nowhere, I was swooped off my feet. Wrapping my arms around Kade's neck, I rested my head on his chest.

"I have no problem with that," I whispered.

He chuckled and carried me into my room and gently set me on the bed.

"Thank you," I said.

"You're welcome. You sure you don't need help?"

"I'm sure. I've got this."

"Good. I'll see you soon," he chimed.

"See you soon," I whispered, as he walked out the door.

I jumped off the bed and limped to the bathroom. *Dang it.* My knee was bruised and it was throbbing. I removed Kade's make-shift tourniquet and replaced it with anti-bacterial ointment and a bandage. After, I went to the dresser and realized I didn't have a bathing suit. Lia packed my bags with warm winter things, not summer things.

"Knock-knock," Lia said, stepping into the room. She looked at me and shook her head. "What happened to you?"

"I fell coming up the stairs," I groaned.

"Are *you* serious? Well, I brought you something. I figured you'd need this." Lia held up a bright-pink, two-piece bikini.

"Are you serious?" I gasped.

"It was either pink, or black with pink polka-dots. I know you don't do polka-dots," she said.

"Nope. But if this is your suit, it's not going to fit me," I stated.

"It'll fit, you'll see. Now march into that bathroom and change," she demanded, pointing at the door. I begrudgingly obliged.

I had worn bathing suits to the beach in L.A. all the time, but there were always tons of other scantily clad beach-goers, which made me feel more comfortable. Here, it was just a few of us, and even fewer women in bikinis.

In the bathroom, I slid the bathing suit on, and damn...Lia was right. It fit perfectly. I turned to the mirror and glanced at myself. Not too bad.

I pulled my hair up into a ponytail, and let a few strands fall to the sides. Lia knocked and as soon as I unlocked the door, she opened it.

Her jaw dropped. "I told you it would fit. Oh my god, Emma. You look freaking hot. Like bathing suit model hot."

"Whatever!" I said, grabbing a towel and wrapping it around me. I didn't like drawing attention to myself, and this bathing suit was a definite attention-getter. I quickly threw on some jeans shorts and a t-shirt.

"Girl, if you got it, you should definitely flaunt it. If I had legs like you, I'd constantly be doing the catwalk walk, like all the time. Work it," she said. She began to walk the length of my room like a supermodel.

"What the heck are you doing?" Jeremy said, opening the door and popping in.

"Pretending like I'm Emma," Lia said, with a hand on her hip, popping her hips side to side with each step. "I'm sexy and I know it," she began to sing.

"What?" Jeremy squeaked.

"Relax. Don't hurt yourself, hun. You had to be here," she said, flicking her hair behind her.

Jeremy scoffed and rolled his eyes. "Well everyone is at the bottom of the stairs. You guys better hurry up."

I grabbed my towel, sunscreen, and sunglasses, and threw them into a backpack.

"Ready?" I said, holding my arm out to Lia.

"Always." She linked hers around mine.

We both sang and did the yellow-brick-road dance from the Wizard of Oz, as we headed out the door. "We're off to see…"

"Yes, you're both off, but couldn't you *try* to be normal for one day?" Jeremy interrupted.

"Normal is lame and boring, especially when we are supah-stahs!" Lia dropped down on one knee and flew both of her arms up into the air with jazz hands.

I started cracking up, and Jeremy had obviously had all he could take.

"Oh my God. You're embarrassing me," he huffed.

"Jeremy, you sound just like my mother, and there are many reasons why I didn't invite her on this trip. So please, give me my moment of freedom and let me live out loud," she said with a serious face, waving her finger at him.

"Whatever, weirdo."

"Oh, I love that song!" Lia exasperated.

"What?" Jeremy twisted back to her.

"Never mind," she grinned and winked at me.

"We love you, Jeremy," I called after him.

"Yeah right," he muttered.

FIFTEEN

ALAINE MUST HAVE GIVEN THE gang all the details because they were packed and ready to go. Malachi was in long jeans shorts, and had a black tank-top on. His tanned muscles bulged and were shining like he'd rubbed oil over himself. He had his signature dark Oakley sunglasses on, making him look even more sinister than usual.

Dominic had on board shorts, and a white t-shirt that made his green eyes glow. Kade walked out from around the corner and also had on swim shorts on with a white tank-top. The chiseled definition of his arms and shoulders was drool-worthy. His chocolate-brown hair was drawn back and his hazel eyes beamed as they landed on me. He threw me a private air kiss.

"Oh heck, Emma. You are so lucky. Can I come live with you?" Lia whispered.

I smiled. If she only knew what living her entailed, she probably wouldn't have even come to visit.

"Let's load up," Alaine said cheerfully.

"Your aunt is beautiful, and you seriously look a lot like her," Lia admitted.

She had on a sleek, one piece bathing suit, with a long, colorful sarong wrapped around her waist. Her hair was pulled back into a long ponytail and she wore a large brimmed hat and sunglasses. She *did* look like royalty.

We loaded into one Hummer. The other was off to the side, and the side door was open.

I wondered how Ethon was going to get there, or if he even agreed. Actually, I knew he would, especially if it involved my safety. Now that I thought about it, he would most likely be flying there.

When we arrived at the lake, it was even more beautiful than I expected. In my mind, I pictured a large muddy hole, filled with water and fish trying to suck the life out of me. But the lake was bigger than I imagined, and actually looked like a real lake. There was sand placed around the edges, making it look beach-like. Manicured grass butted up to the sand, and beyond that, were beautiful spruce and birch trees.

I was a gorgeous setting. Two small row boats were set on the beach, and in another corner was a volleyball net. On the far side of the bank, I noticed a large birch tree with a fat rope tied to one of its branches.

"Wow. This place is amazing," Lia said as she stepped out of the vehicle.

Our party consisted of Alaine, Dominic, Malachi, Kade, Courtney, Caleb, Jeremy, Lia and me.

I knew our extra backup wasn't too far behind.

Warmth and tingling pricks shot across my skin, causing me to pause. Ethon was here. I glanced around and saw nothing. But I knew he was out there, hidden in the shadows of the trees.

I hoped today would be Lucian free, but I always expected the worse. Prepare for the worst, and hope for the best. That was my new motto. These days, when we least expected it, it usually happened. That had become the story of my life. But at least we were prepared.

Alaine laid out a large blanket on the grass and set up a chair with an umbrella. She looked like she'd done this a few times before and was completely prepared.

As soon as Dominic jumped out of the car he ripped his shirt off.

Lia grabbed my arm and squeezed as she watched him run to the rope swing. He was perfection…but they all were.

Lia and Courtney stripped down to their bathing suits and headed for the water.

Jeremy also took his shirt off and followed after Dominic. His lean, non-muscular body looked awkward as he hobbled over the heated sand toward the rope swing. Caleb kept his shirt and shorts on, sitting in the sand, watching Lia and Courtney.

"Come in, Caleb," Lia called. He paused, then slowly got up, took his shirt off, and jumped - splashing water all over them. The girls screamed and a water fight began.

I laughed, happy to see them having fun.

Malachi carried his chair to a nice shady spot on the lake and set himself up. He had a small cooler with drinks and snacks. He looked pretty cool with his dark shades on. Maybe, if everything went well, he could get a nap in like he'd wanted to.

It was just me and Kade left.

"Would you like to take a boat out onto the lake with me?" I asked.

"Sure," he smiled.

He pulled his shirt off, and headed for the boat.

Lia did a double take as she noticed him walk by. Her head snapped over to me with wide eyes.

I smiled and laughed inside. Yep. He was perfect, and he was mine. But then I noticed something I never saw before. His back was covered with scars from the burns, and I suddenly had a horrible flashback.

It all seemed like an unbelievable nightmare, but the sight of his scars brought it all back, making it real. My eyes misted over. His scars. The pain he endured. They were an outward sign of his love for me, and a realization of what he did. He risked his life to save mine. He protected me, and for that, his scars had become his most beautiful feature. A perfect reminder of everything he was to me.

He pulled the boat into the water and jumped in, glancing up at me. "Coming?" he asked holding his hand out. I nodded and smiled, discreetly wiping away the tear which escaped my eye.

"Take it off, Emma!" Lia hollered. I glared at her, and shook my head. "Girl, if you don't take it off, I'll come up there and rip it off." Her eyes were locked and narrowed, and I knew she would do just as she said. She never made idle threats. Lia *always* followed through.

I sighed and reluctantly pulled off my top and then slowly slipped off my shorts.

Every eye darted to the bright pink.

Dammit. I suddenly felt naked.

There was a loud whistle from across the lake. Dominic.

"Looking hot, Emma!" he yelled. He was standing on one of the branches of the big tree.

I shook my head, my face flushed with the heat of embarrassment. I quickly made my way toward the boat, and hopped inside. A crooked grin formed on Kade's lips as he carefully appraised me.

"Beautiful," he breathed.

"Thank you. But it's not mine."

"I wasn't talking about the suit."

I blushed, if I could blush any more than I already had. Taking my seat opposite of Kade, he grabbed the oars and began to row us out into the middle of the lake. I was hoping we could spend some time alone out there.

"Hey! If you guys want to see something totally awesome, I suggest you look this way," Dominic announced on the largest, highest branch of the tree. With the rope in hand, he jumped, dropping down and flying outward, traveling at a crazy speed. As he reached his highest point, he let go and tucked his legs, spinning... one, two, three, four, *five* times before hitting the water with a splash.

"Holy shit!" Jeremy cursed.

Everyone started clapping, except Malachi, whose head was

tilted forward. He was probably asleep.

Jeremy was freaking out, clapping and cheering. I watched as he started to climb the tree, and highly doubted he could do one, let alone half a flip.

We all watched as Jeremy climbed to the largest limb, and grabbed hold of the rope.

"Don't hurt yourself," Lia yelled. She had to. She was a mother-hen.

Jeremy hesitated.

"Are you chickening out?" Lia laughed.

He glanced down toward her. "Never," he yelled, and pushed off the branch. He swung awkwardly out over the lake, and a high pitched scream loudly followed after him. I found myself laughing, but as soon as he reached the highest point, he didn't let go.

His eyes were shut.

"Jeremy, let go!" I bellowed, standing up, my heart pounding. But he didn't listen, and hugged tighter to the rope.

"Let go you idiot!" Lia yelled, trying to run in the water toward him. Everyone started to scream at him to let go, but he had become one with the rope.

Dominic started to swim toward him, and Malachi jumped from his chair and started running. Even Alaine was headed his way.

"He's gonna hit the tree!" I screamed, slapping my hands over my mouth. My heart sunk as I helplessly watched him flying backward towards the tree, at a speed which could knock him out, or possibly injure him badly. My breath seized.

An instant wave of electricity buzzed around me, and the leaves begin to rustle. Then, with a sudden strong gust of wind, and a blink of an eye later, Jeremy was magically off the rope, and safely on the ground.

He stood there, eyes still closed...screaming. That is, until he realized he was safe. When his eyes opened, they were wide, dazed and confused.

Lia pointed to him. "How did—? What the—? Did anyone see that?" She stuttered.

"I think he let go," Courtney answered, also confused.

"That was some crazy crap right there. How the hell did he get on the ground? He should have smacked that tree," Lia exhaled, her hands grasping the sides of her head.

I knew exactly what happened. Ethon saved him. He was the only one who could fly that fast.

I shook my head and smiled, exhaling a sigh of relief. Thank goodness he was safe.

"Jeremy, step away from the rope and get your geeky butt back over here where it's safe," Lia scolded.

Jeremy didn't even give a retort; he just stumbled away from the tree. Alaine finally reached him, and wrapped her arm around his shoulder, assisting him back to the bank.

I slumped back into the boat.

"He was pretty lucky," Kade said.

"Yeah," I breathed.

"I take it your friend hasn't swung from a rope before."

"Nope, and I don't think he ever will again," I sighed.

Dominic suddenly popped up and grabbed hold of the side of

the boat, scaring the crap out of me.

"Dom, you can't do that," I exasperated, reaching out and lightly smacking the top of his head.

"Emma, our orders were to guard and protect from any Fallen or Darkling. Protecting your friends from themselves wasn't part of the deal. I'm just letting you know, that'll be extra."

"Well, you'd better start a tab...but if we happen to encounter any Hellhounds in the near future, I'll be sure to save your ass, and we can call it even," I winked.

"*Burn*! She got you good man," Kade laughed.

"Touché," Dominic nodded, with a huge smile on his face. "You're pretty witty, Emma. I think I might be rubbing off on you."

"Yeah, and that's not necessarily a good thing," Kade said, pushing him away.

"Don't be jealous, dude. Green's not your color," Dominic teased, as he sunk under the water and disappeared.

"I wonder if we'll ever get a moment of peace today," I said. I could still feel the heavy beating of my heart.

"That's highly doubtful. It was only what...five minutes before we encountered our first mishap? I think we all need to be on full alert today," Kade answered.

"I think you're right," I admitted.

Turning around, I watched Lia laugh as she talked with Courtney and Caleb. Jeremy soon joined them, and before long, they started a game of shoulder wrestling. Lia jumped onto Caleb's shoulders, and Courtney was on Jeremy's. They wrestled, laughed, and screamed. In no time, Jeremy and Courtney were in the water.

Caleb and Lia cheered, rubbing it in. Lia might have had a small frame, but she was freakishly strong for her size.

"Don't you want to be with your friends?" Kade asked.

"By the looks of it, I'd be the odd girl out. Unless you'd like to join me?" I glanced at him.

"For you, yes. But no physical contact games...unless they're with you."

"That could be arranged," I teased.

He turned the boat around and as he rowed toward the others, Thomas and Alexander showed up. They must have parked down the road to avoid the same-car-confusion.

This was still going to be hard to explain.

I knew Jeremy and Lia would, sooner or later, know something was up. How could they not when there were perfect guys, with perfect bodies, and gorgeous faces, who seemed to pop up all around us.

Jeremy would definitely question it, but Lia...she would cancel her flight and live with me. I glanced over and watched her mouth gape as she noticed them. Alexander looked our age. He had short, raven hair, and dark eyes. Thomas had blond hair and baby blue eyes. The Guardians were strikingly masculine, with angular, angelic features and magnetic personalities.

"Oh my God. I think I've died and gone to heaven" Lia said, doe-eyed, fanning herself.

"Well, you're close," Courtney giggled. Caleb gave her a shooting glance, which she shrugged off.

I laughed and turned to Kade who even cracked a smile.

"I think she's a bit overwhelmed, and I have a feeling she'll be begging me to stay."

"You can always assure her there will be future visits."

"That's true. But the one I'm really worried about is Jeremy. I know him. He's probably speculating and forming a hypothesis. I just hope it concludes with an indecisive answer."

I turned to Jeremy and watched his eyes sweep over each of the Guardians, studying and scrutinizing. Samuel and James never showed, and I was glad. I knew they were out there, just choosing to remain hidden with Ethon and the goons.

"Hey friends," Thomas called, waving to us.

"Hello!" Dominic chided. "You are welcome to come and swim in our lake, but to enter you must use the rope."

"I assume you have?" Alexander yelled.

"Yes. Five spins," he answered.

Both Thomas and Alexander smiled widely. The everlasting competition continued, and looks of determination and impending victory were embedded on each face. Dropping their things on the grass, they sprinted toward the tree.

Thomas climbed up first. His surfer-boy, beach-body flexed as he grabbed the rope. He started from the middle of the branch, ran, and jumped. His body shot out like a rocket, the rope thrusting him out and up. He let go, spreading his arms like a bird, and then as he started to drop, he tucked in and spun. He moved so fast, I couldn't keep track.

Dominic cursed, and as soon as Thomas hit the water, everyone was silent.

"*O.M.G.* Are these guys for real?" Lia exhaled loudly.

"They must be divers," Caleb said. Jeremy looked at him, with his eyes narrowed.

"Yeah, freaking world-class Olympic divers," Lia added.

"Seven," Thomas yelled, as his head broke the water.

"Seven? That's it?" Alexander teased.

"Mortals over here!" I shouted, glaring up at him. I had to remind them that there were humans present.

"What was that, Emma?" Lia asked.

"Sorry. I was just reminding them that we are but mere mortals over here, so they should stop showing off," I babbled.

"You're so strange," she laughed.

"I'm sure you can do a bunch of flips, but let's keep it safe. I don't want to be liable for injuries," Alaine added.

"Fine," Alexander sighed. He grabbed the rope and jumped, swinging out over the lake and did a one flip and then bombed Thomas and Dominic.

"Do you know them?" Jeremy asked.

"Neighbors," Alaine answered. "I've given them permission to use the lake as long as they are safe and keep it in good condition.

"That's nice of you," Jeremy noted.

"I try and keep good relations with all of my neighbors. When you are so far from civilization, you have to rely on those around you for help. Everyone is willing to give a hand when needed. You learn to become very resourceful out here."

"That's a wise concept to have," Jeremy added.

"It is. We have wonderful friends and neighbors surrounding us."

"That's a good thing," Lia added.

"That's a very good thing," Alaine smiled.

"I really like it here," Lia said. "Emma is really lucky to have you. I'm glad I won't have to worry about her so much anymore."

"Well, we have been blessed to have her here. She's been a missing link for so long, and having her here has made my life complete," Alaine said, placing her glasses back over her eyes. "And we are very happy that you came to visit her. She will definitely need your support tomorrow."

"What's tomorrow?" Courtney asked.

"The funeral," Caleb whispered.

"Oh," she whispered back.

I hadn't realized I froze, until Kade grabbed my hand.

"Hey. You okay?"

"Yeah," I blew a slow breath out. "I still can't believe their gone." I knew the day would come, but I wasn't prepared for it.

"I'm here for you," he said.

"I know."

SIXTEEN

"**E**MMA, GET YOUR BRIGHT-PINK booty over here. We're going to play beach volleyball."

"Oh, I don't know if you can handle our team," I laughed.

"Alright, how about you and Kade against the rest of us?" she asked.

"That's not fair," Kade said, jumping out of the boat. He offered his hand to help me out, then pushed it to the shore. I went and grabbed the volleyball.

"Well, we can hand you over, Courtney," Caleb said. She shot him an evil glare.

"That's not what he meant. He meant it's not fair…for the rest of you," I said.

"Oh, I see how it is. Just diss your BFF's while they visit," Lia rolled her eyes. "Well, for your information, my fabulous friend, we have brains *and* brawn," she said flexing.

"Bring it," I said. I pulled my shorts back on, and threw on my t-shirt. I didn't want a wardrobe malfunction, or to see body parts flying about. That would have been embarrassing. Kade also put on his tank top, and I was glad. His abs would have been a major distraction, especially for Lia.

The four of them set up on one side, and Kade and I on the other.

"We got this," he winked. I nodded.

Caleb hit the ball over the net and it went right between us. I ran, he ran, and when he saw that I was coming, he stopped. I missed the ball and fell forward, landing on top of him.

"Yes! Our point," Courtney squealed.

"I'm so sorry! Is your back okay?" I asked.

"Yeah right! You totally did that on purpose," Lia yelled.

"I'm fine," Kade laughed, placing his hands on either side of my waist.

"You guys can get up now," Jeremy huffed.

I jumped up.

"I think I'll let you get the next one," I said.

Caleb hit the ball and right as it came over the net, Kade jumped up and spiked it down, right between Caleb and Jeremy. Sand flew everywhere and they stood frozen, wide-eyed at the power.

"What just happened?" Lia said.

"Point!" I exclaimed, high-fiving Kade. "Take that!"

"Do all the people who live in Alaska play Olympic-style sports? I didn't even *see* the ball after he touched it."

"I need some water," Jeremy said.

"I'll go grab the cooler," Kade said, running toward the cooler at the other end of the lake.

Caleb was teaching Jeremy how to serve, when he whacked the ball into the trees.

"Great, Jeremy!" Lia scolded.

"I'll get it," I laughed.

"No, I'll get it, Emma," Jeremy said.

"Jeremy, you've had enough adventure," Lia blurted. "You'd get lost and we'd have to search for your lost butt."

"I know where it landed. I'll be right back." I laughed. I watched it land about twenty feet back. As I made my way into the trees, I didn't see it. I swear I saw it land in this spot.

Then, when I looked further back, it was another fifteen yards in.

"Dammit, Jeremy," I breathed, pushing past some thick brush. When I was about ten feet away, a dark figure stepped out from the trees, his back facing me.

My heart dropped, and a cold shiver rushed through me.

Fallen.

How the hell did he get past the others? This place must have been too big to cover.

His back was still facing me as he bent over and picked up the ball. When he stood, he held the ball out to the side of him. "Are you looking for this?" His voice made every single hair on my body stand.

"What do you want?" I asked, my voice shaking. I had nothing on, or around me, to defend myself.

"You know exactly what I want." His head snapped around. My breath hitched. His eyes were completely black.

"No, I don't," I said, slowly backing up.

"Take one more step back, or scream, and I'll take your head off," he threatened. His words dripped with malice. He was tall and thinner than most Fallen I'd seen, and his features were angular and sharp. Stringy dark brown hair hung over half his face, and down past his shoulders. In one hand, he held the ball. In the other, a very sharp, long sword.

"I haven't done anything to you," I said, trying to keep myself alive as long as possible.

"Not yet... Nephilim," he hissed, spitting out the word like it tasted bad.

There was a rustling in the trees to the side of me, and when I turned, another dark figure stepped out of the brush. As I opened my mouth to scream, a large hand flew over my mouth, stifling my cries. His other arm wrapped around my chest. He was big, and brawny, but I was not going to die without a fight.

I kicked my legs, thrusting them against the trees and against the knees and thighs of my assailant, and dug my nails into his hands and face, struggling to free myself.

I tried to bite him, but his hand was locked so tight I couldn't open my mouth.

He cursed and squeezed until my lungs ached and my ribs cracked. Pain shot through my chest.

I suddenly froze as he raised a dagger and placed it to my throat.

He pressed hard enough for me to feel a sting, and then I felt a warm trickling drip down my neck.

Bastard.

I dared not move, because if I struggled, the blade would slice through even deeper. I felt my eyes water, but I held it back. I wouldn't give him the satisfaction of watching me become weak.

The one holding the ball stepped forward. "Lucian wants you alive, but it will be so much easier to take you dead. We could say it was an accident. But, before we leave, maybe we can have some fun."

He was vile and repulsive. His teeth were corroded and when he came close, his stench burned my nostrils. I fought to keep the bile from rising in my chest, but I couldn't turn away from him for fear the blade would slice deeper.

He stepped even closer to me, placing his nose near the nape of my neck and deeply inhaled.

What the hell was up with the smelling? Freaking freak.

"Your scent makes my mouth water. Makes me want to taste you," he hissed.

He stuck out an abnormally long tongue, and licked his lips. He then lowered his head and pressed his slimy serpentine tongue to my neck, sliding it upward, leaving a trail of nauseating wet across the side of my face.

You freaking disgusting bastard! I'd like to wrap that tongue around your neck and squeeze the life out of you.

His blackened eyes felt like daggers as he glared at me. A sudden dark, sickening feeling of horror filled my insides. I closed my eyes, wishing it would end.

"Open your eyes, Nephilim," the Fallen exhaled in a wicked whisper. "There is nothing like watching a life extinguish from one's eyes."

An instant wave of dizziness rushed over me as he raised his sword to kill me.

Death. I knew it was inevitable, but not now. Not this way.

Kade, Ethon, where are you?

My thoughts went to my Guardian, who was unable to save me. He would be heart broken.

I blinked as the Fallen thrust his sword forward to pierce my heart, but the blade never met its mark. Instead, it stopped and fell to the ground, along with a severed arm.

Before the Fallen realized he had lost a limb, his eyes widened. He tried to speak, or scream, but nothing, not even a whisper left his lips. His words and breath were trapped inside of him.

I watched as a cold, white frost writhed its way from the edges of his eyes until they were fully changed. His head fell forward, off his shoulders, and tumbled to the ground. His body was not too far behind, dropping with a thud. As it did, electric warmth blanketed me, filling me with a sense of hope.

Standing in place of the Fallen, holding a blood-covered sword, was Ethon. His eyes were blazing with a rage I'd never witnessed before. They were savage and blood-thirsty. His face was hard-set with murderous intent, dark and fixed on my attacker.

"You hold my mate in your grasp, Fallen. Release the blade from her neck, or I will cut your fingers off, one by one, and feed them to you before I rip your head off," he slowly threatened.

My heart thrummed as I focused on him, but his eyes never left his target. He was beautifully terrifying. The way he stood and held his sword – angled downward but slightly tilted to the side; the way stray strands of his raven hair wisped over his fiery eyes; the way he spoke – with a quiet intimidation.

My dark knight had arrived.

"Ethon. Traitor…" the Fallen growled, holding the blade in place. "If your father finds out what you've done—"

"My father *sent* me," a wicked sneer grew on his lips.

I could feel the thunderous beat of the Fallen's heart against my back. His breath became ragged, but I remained frozen, knowing with one quick press, my life would end.

Ethon remained cool and motionless. The calm before the storm.

"Now…one last time. Release her, and I'll make your death quick and painless. Fail to do it immediately and you will die slowly and painfully. It's your choice," Ethon stated, matter-of-factly.

I was suddenly released from the Fallen's crushing grip. Excruciating pain shot through my chest and ribs as I inhaled. My weak legs gave way. But before I hit the ground, Ethon flew forward, decapitating the Fallen, and catching me in his arms.

The flame in his eyes instantly extinguished, as his attention aimed on my injuries.

"Emma, why are you here unprotected?" he breathed, dropping his sword to the ground.

"I was getting the volleyball."

"The what?" he questioned.

"Never mind," I breathed. "Thank you. For saving me."

"It was nothing," he said, his eyes suddenly narrowed with concern. "Your neck. It's bleeding."

"It's fine. It'll heal, eventually." I placed my hand to my neck and when I lifted, it was soaked with blood. I exhaled and a sharp pain radiated through my side. "I think I have some broken ribs."

"I can help. It might burn a bit, but it will stop the bleeding and mend any fractures," he said.

"Okay," I nodded, knowing that if anyone saw seeping blood from my throat, it would be a freak-out fest. "Please, do it."

Ethon carefully laid me down, and moved directly to my side. He closed his eyes, and put himself into some sort of trance. Smoke started to smolder from the crevices of his eyes. When his eyelids snapped open, they were burning…actual flames danced around in place of his eyes. He raised his hands in front of him, and they began to glow like red hot coals.

I braced myself, remembering how painful it was when Malachi fixed my broken ribs in the airport.

First, he gently placed his right hand over the wound, and heat instantly spread through the opening. I endured the pain, but it was only for a few seconds. He then moved to my mid-section. Heat filled the area and soon the sharp pains diminished to a dull ache.

He closed his eyes again, and when they opened, they were back to their normal color. He glanced at my neck and a slight grin formed on his face as he appraised his work.

"It'll be a few days before the scar goes away, but at least the wound is closed. Your ribs will be sore for a while longer, so try to keep activities to a minimum. Okay?" He bent down and placed a light kiss over the new scar on my neck, and then left another one on my nose, as he sat back up.

I smiled, admiring his tenderness. "I have to say, you're pretty incredible."

His crimson eyes raised and met mine, and a look of playfulness flickered.

"Incredible enough to bond with?" he smirked.

"Don't push it," I laughed. "I'm in complete awe of everything you did for me. I'm really glad you were here. And I also wanted to say thank you, again, for saving my friend. He could have been badly injured."

His grin grew a little larger. "You knew it was me?"

"Of course. No one else could fly that fast," I said.

He puffed. "I only did it for you. I could care less about your dimwitted friend."

"He's not dimwitted. He's actually very book smart. Just not very...outdoorsy."

We were both snapped back into reality with loud yelling.

"Emma! Emma!" Lia and Courtney's voices were frantic calling out for me.

"Let's get you out of here," Ethon said. He stood and bent down, lifting me up, cradling in his arms.

It felt like I'd been here for a very long time, but in actuality, I'd been gone for no more than a couple minutes. Both of the Fallen's bodies had burned, incinerating themselves into ash. I should have been going crazy at this point, but this was my new life.

As we exited the woods, everyone was already rushing in our direction. I saw Samuel step out from the trees, but Alaine motioned to him. She must have reassured him everything was okay, and then I watched her give him a signal to keep watch. He ducked back into the trees and Malachi followed.

"Oh my goodness, Emma. What the hell happened to you?" Lia asked. Her eyes went wide as she looked up to Ethon. "Where the hell did this guy come from? And why the hell is he carrying you? Is that blood? How did you get hurt?" She gasped, and almost started to hyperventilate.

"Slow down, Lia. I'm fine," I put my hand back around his neck. "This is Ethon."

She took in a deep breath and exhaled slowly. "So, is Ethon another neighbor?" she questioned, shaking her head in disbelief.

"I am," Ethon answered. "I live just down the way."

"He actually lives way further down," Dominic said, coming up from behind him and slapping him on the shoulder. "Like, way down."

Ethon shot him a fiery glare.

I watched Thomas and Alexander quickly slip into the trees. They were probably going to make sure it was all clear.

"Whoa. Do you have red eyes?" Jeremy asked, immediately taking notice of Ethon.

"They're contacts," Ethon quickly responded. "It's the newest thing. The red completely blocks the UV out, and makes everything look pretty freaking awesome."

"Whoa, I'm totally going to get some of those," Lia said. "You should get some too, Jeremy, but you'd probably scare everyone. The geek-creature, complete with bushy hair and red eyes."

Jeremy rolled his eyes at her.

Ethon set me down, just as Kade reached us.

"Emma, what happened?" His brow was furrowed with concern. "I went to get the cooler, and on the way back they were yelling your name. You were just gone, and I had no clue where you went."

"Yeah, some Guardian," Ethon huffed. "But don't worry, I kept her safe. She doesn't need you anymore, not that you're very effective in the first place."

"Bastard," Kade cursed, his eyes narrowed as he stepped forward, challenging Ethon.

"Stop, please." I stepped in between them and pushed them apart. "It's no one's fault but mine. I shouldn't have gone in the woods alone. I should have told someone. It was a stupid move. I was just going to get the ball, and it ended up being further away than I thought."

"Emma," Kade breathed, shaking his head. I could tell he was crushed he wasn't there to protect me.

I lifted my hand and placed it over his chest, then looked into his pained eyes. "I'm sorry. I promise never to do anything stupid like that again."

He laid his hand over mine and exhaled. "I'm just glad you're safe." He then turned to Ethon, "And for that, I thank you."

I knew it took a lot for Kade to speak those words. But before I could see Ethon's response Alaine stepped in and pulled me away.

"Emma, you should never go anywhere unattended," she said,

wrapping a towel around me. "What happened?" Her fingers ran across the area the Fallen placed the blade.

"Did he touch you?" Kade asked. I wondered if Ethon's hand had left a mark.

"No. It's not like that. I promise. I'll tell you the entire story when we get home, okay?"

"What story? What's going on?" Jeremy questioned.

My heart sank and my head started to ache. This was the very thing I was trying to avoid.

"Yeah. Emma, why do you need protection? What happened in the woods?" Lia questioned.

Courtney and Caleb stayed in the background. They knew to keep quiet, but I could tell they were just as confused.

I had to come up with some kind of story. "Well, there were...two bears in the woods, but Ethon killed them." *Oh for the love of God...bears?* My explanation was so weak, and I sounded like an idiot attempting to make up a campfire story for five-year olds. "I'm fine. Really," I assured them.

"Bears? Are you kidding me? No one said there were bears here," Lia exclaimed, her eyes became wide in terror as they shot to the woods. She quickly moved to the opposite side of Jeremy.

"What did he kill them with? I didn't hear a gun," Jeremy asked. He looked at us intently.

I hesitated too long. "His...sword," I said very slowly, my voice going up at the end.

But I had no choice. I couldn't keep lying to them.

"A sword? He killed two bears with a sword?" I could tell

Jeremy was having a hard time trying to wrap his mind around that explanation.

"I did," Ethon confirmed. "I slayed the beasts with my sword. It was quite impressive."

I exhaled and grinned, happy he came to my rescue, again.

"Don't tell me. Olympic fencing?" Lia questioned.

"Excuse me?" Ethon looked at her blankly.

"Don't mind her. She's obsessed with the Olympics," Courtney muttered.

"I think we should pack up and head home," Alaine said.

"Yes, I think we should leave, like five minutes ago," Lia said, quickly making a beeline for her things.

Malachi returned and helped us load the car, while Dominic, Thomas, and Alexander questioned Ethon. I watched as he told his story and pointed to the area, and then they all followed him into the woods.

As I was placing my backpack in the back of the car, Malachi came and stood beside me, shaking his head.

"I know, I know. You don't have to rub it in," I said.

"I wasn't going to. Just be sure to let one of us know if you ever feel the need to wander. We can't protect you, if we don't know where you are."

I glanced up at him, but was met with his dark glasses. "I will. I promise."

He placed his hand on my shoulder. "Glad you're okay."

"Thanks."

We were all accounted for as we loaded into the Hummer, but

we weren't home yet. Courtney, Lia, Caleb, and Jeremy seemed to find an easy friendship. I was happy for them, but became sad as I started to feel a bit of disconnect. I knew it was inevitable. I was different now. They were one hundred percent mortal, and weren't prepared for my new world. How could they be, when I still wasn't?

Just a few months ago, things were so different. So simple. I never really had any worries, and lived life carefree. But things changed quickly after the accident. Jeremy and Lia didn't belong in this new world of death and destruction. They weren't safe around me anymore, and it broke my heart.

My insides were still trembling from the incident in the woods, but I dared not show it. Especially in front of them. I almost died today, but my friends would never know. They could *never* know.

I wondered how those Fallen were able to get so close. I was glad that no one else entered the woods. Things could have ended much worse than it did. I couldn't let anything happen to my friends. I wouldn't allow it. I had to keep them close and safe, under the confines of the barrier until they returned home. But that was easier said than done. I guess I could pull the bear card. That would definitely keep Lia inside.

Kade wrapped his arm around me and pulled me against him. I grabbed his hand, interlacing my fingers through his, and laid my head on his shoulder. I felt his warm breath on my forehead as he pressed his cheek to the side of it, and I was instantly comforted.

Home wasn't far, but he and I sat in silence - both of our minds reeling with unanswered questions. Although my world felt like it was falling apart, I knew he would be there to steady me.

SEVENTEEN

AFTER DINNER, PLANS WERE ALREADY set and I didn't even have a say. All of the humans and I were going to Courtney's room for movies. Kade graciously declined, saying I needed to spend time with them without distraction. I made him feel bad by giving the puppy dog eyes, but he was right. I only had a few more days with them.

Courtney had already set up popcorn, an assortment of candies, and a cooler of drinks leftover from the lake. Her room was just as spacious as mine was, and everything was set up on a big fluffy area rug in the center of the room.

On the wall hung a sixty inch flat screen television with surround sound. I didn't even have a TV in my room, but I guess I didn't need one. Courtney spent a lot of her free time here. She deserved it.

They decided on an all-night movie marathon, with none other than...dun-duh-duh-duuun... The Lord of the Rings trilogy.

Shocking.

We were all ordered to wear jammies, and bring our own pillows.

"Come on, Emma," Lia said, patting the space beside her. She had on a Hello Kitty onesie.

I smiled and plopped down as Courtney pressed play.

As soon as it started, the room shook.

"Whoa. This surround sound is awesome," Jeremy yelled above the noise.

Courtney smiled and nodded.

The movie was playing, and as much as I tried to keep my head in the moment, it kept drifting away. As soon as an apple hit a character's head, I suddenly wanted one. I knew there were big, crisp, juicy apples in the house, but they were all the way downstairs in the fridge. The popcorn was too buttery and left a weird film on the top of my mouth, and the candy wasn't the kind of sweet I craved.

I mean, who has a party without peppermint candy canes?

I debated with myself for about five minutes because I didn't want to make the long trip to the kitchen, but also didn't want any snacks here either.

I stood, and Courtney pressed paused.

"I'm craving an apple. I'm going to the kitchen to get one. Anyone need anything?" I asked.

"An apple? Are you kidding me? Healthy snacks are not allowed on movie nights," Lia said, shaking her head.

"Well, I'm craving one. So do you need anything, or not?"

It was a resounding no.

"Fine," I said. "Courtney, please press play. I could practically recite this movie, word for word."

"Are you sure?" she asked.

"Positive," I stressed.

"Alright," she shrugged. She pressed play and the blast of volume made everyone jump. I heard them laughing as I made my way into the hall, shutting the door behind me.

I quickly made my way downstairs and headed for the kitchen. As I turned down the hall, I noticed the light was on, and then heard voices. I quietly snuck forward and peeked in. It was Thomas and Alexander. They were rummaging in the fridge.

"Hey guys," I loudly announced.

They both popped up, and Alexander cracked his head on the fridge.

"Ouch, dammit," he cursed, rubbing his head.

"I'm so sorry!" I apologized. "I didn't mean to scare you."

"No, you didn't scare us," Thomas noted, with a smile. "You startled us."

"Oh, okay. Well, I'm sorry for *startling* you. So what are you guys doing in here?"

"Raiding the kitchen for food. Miss Lily said we could have whatever we wanted, and our place is empty," Alexander said, grabbing plastic containers, filled with leftovers. "Muffins. Score!" he cheered, taking out a large baggie labeled blueberry muffins.

"Our place is empty because someone is constantly eating, every-second-of-every-day," Thomas sighed.

"Yeah, dude. You better cut that crap out," Alexander said, heading to the cupboard and taking out a bag of chips and another bag of chocolate chip cookies. He placed it in their sack, which topped it off.

"So, what are you doing down here, Emma?" Thomas asked.

"I wanted an apple. The rest of them are upstairs having a movie marathon, and I just can't seem to get into it."

"I don't blame you. You went through a lot today. I'm surprised you can still function at all," Thomas said. He threw some peanuts into his mouth.

"It's hard, but I think tomorrow will be worse," I sighed.

"Why?" Alexander asked, chomping down on a cookie.

"Dude, funeral…" Thomas nudged him.

Alexander froze and turned to me with sad eyes. "Oh. I'm sorry, Emma. We might not be there, but our hearts will be with you."

"Thank you so much. I just can't wait until all of this is over."

"We all can't wait," Thomas agreed, "for your and Alaine's sake."

I suddenly realized the reason they were here with us. It never really crossed my mind before. I mean, I knew they were here as Guardians on assignment, but that was it. They were only assigned. Once this mission was complete…it was over.

What would this house be like when they were all gone? No Dominic, Thomas, Alexander or Malachi? It would be empty.

My heart wrenched, and sadness overtook me. They had become a huge part of my family - a vital part to my existence. They all helped to fill the void, and brought life to this place.

"So what will happen to all of you, once this is all over?" I asked.

"We'll go back to Midway and wait for our next mission," Thomas answered.

I nodded and swallowed the lump in my throat, trying to fight my emotions.

"So how many more years before each of you get your wings?" I questioned.

They glanced at each other.

"Kade explained to me how it all works. I know about the coins, and the five hundred years."

"I have two hundred and eighty-five more years of service," Thomas smiled, and raked his fingers through is beach blonde hair.

"And I have three hundred and seventy-six years left," Alexander added.

"He's the baby," Thomas nodded at him, patting his head.

"Dude, don't rub your grimy hands in my silky hair. I just washed it," Alexander huffed. His hair was almost the exact same raven color as Ethon's, only Alexander was clean cut.

I half-heartedly laughed at their banter. "I'm really going to miss you guys when you leave."

"Yeah, no joke. There hasn't been, nor will there ever be, another mission like this one. It has been my favorite mission by far," Alexander said.

"Yeah, same here," Thomas added. "We are usually sent out alone, to protect or watch over one soul at a time. Like how Kade was sent to protect you."

"And I never even had a clue," I whispered.

"The mortals are never aware. But you're lucky. If Kade was still an immortal, he'd also have to leave and return to Midway until his five hundred years were served," Thomas added.

"Even if he was bonded?" I asked.

"Why? Are you planning on bonding with him?" Alexander asked, wiggling his brows.

"Alex, shut-up," Thomas said, slapping his back. "The answer is yes, Emma. Even if he was bonded."

Thinking this new information over, I started to feel a little relief. "So, now that he is mortal...he will get to stay here, with no issues from above?"

"Yes," they both replied.

I nodded. "Well, I guess I better get back up to the gang before they send down a search party." I turned to leave and remembered something.

By the way, how is Samuel holding up?"

"He's doing really well, but has been sleeping a lot because his wings are still healing. Especially after the long flight the other day. But in no time he'll be good-as-new. He'll probably be able to fly without pain in about a month.

"A whole month?" My heart twisted.

"Yeah, those damn Grimlocks did a number on him, but he's living like a king. He hasn't had modern amenities for a while, so he's in hog heaven," Thomas laughed. "Plus, Alaine has been spoiling him."

"That's good. I hope I'll get a chance to see him soon," I said.

"Well, he can't come here with the barrier up, but you are free to come over and visit anytime you like. We've got you covered,"

Thomas winked.

"Thank you," I said.

"Yeah, even the red-eyed demon is out and about, checking the area. We saw him take off on our way here," Alexander added.

I smiled inside, but kept my expression blank and nodded. Ethon was their enemy. The son of Lucifer, who was now bonded to the one they were protecting.

"Well, please tell Samuel I said hello."

"We will," Thomas said. "Hope you have a good night."

Alex was back in the fridge. He peeked out and tossed me a large apple.

"Thank you both. For everything," I said grasping it.

"It's our duty and our pleasure," Thomas winked.

"Yeah, what he said," Alexander blurted, before shoving something crunchy into his mouth.

I smiled and followed behind them as they left, locking the door and clicking the light off. I stood in the dark and glanced into the night sky. The stars gently illuminated the labyrinth and the cottage.

I turned to leave, but gasped at a dark figure standing in the doorway.

"Don't be afraid," he whispered. I stretched my arm to turn on the light, but he stopped me. "Don't. Leave it off." The sound of his voice was so low, so alluring, it sent a rush of warm pricks through my body.

A smile crossed my face as I observed his perfect silhouette. I pressed my back to the door as he stalked closer, only stopping when his firm body was pressed tightly against mine, capturing me.

He put his hands up on either side of me, locking me in place. Then he leaned down, to kiss my neck, making a trail all the way up to my ear.

"What are you doing here in the dark, all alone?" His breath tickled my ear and sent shivers down my spine. Using one hand for support, Kade took the other and firmly grabbed my waist, pulling me against him. Placing his lips over mine, just enough to talk against them, he said, "Are you going to make me ask again?"

"I'm not alone," I whispered. "Not anymore."

He nipped at my bottom lip and then quickly pressed his mouth over mine.

This was so unlike him, and it excited me. "Why are you here?"

"I come down here once in a while..." he punctuated with kisses, "...hoping to run into a girl I met a while back." He sucked the bottom of my lip. "Have you seen her around?"

Parts of me started tingling, so I played along. "I don't know," I replied, kissing him back. "What does this girl look like?"

The heat between us was reaching boiling point, our bodies were now moving against each other of their own accord. Kade, nearly breathless said, "She's young and beautiful. We met here, in this very kitchen. She couldn't sleep, so I offered to use my magic on her. You see, I'm her Guardian, but I haven't been able to find her."

"Maybe she's changed and you just don't recognize her? If you're her Guardian, I'm sure she needs you...badly."

The last thread of his composure disintegrated and his mouth plunged into mine. I dropped my apple and my hands tangled in his hair, holding him against me. For a moment, we were tongues, teeth, and lips…pushing and fighting for dominance.

Kade's powerful hands grabbed onto my hips, and his hard body pushed me forcefully into the door.

Bam!

We both stopped and froze.

"What was that?" I said.

"Shhh…" He turned his head to look, and after a few long seconds, I could feel him start to laugh. "It was just the dishwasher door falling down. It must not have been closed properly."

We looked at each other and broke out into laughter.

The mood was definitely ruined.

"By the way, I know the girl you're speaking of," I said. "We're very close, she and I. As a matter of fact, she spoke very highly of you. Just before you interrupted me tonight, she had told me that you are the glue holding her together. You've filled in the pieces of her broken heart, and were her very first love."

"She told you all of that?" he whispered, as he pressed his forehead against mine.

"Yes."

"Could I tell her something in return?" He asked softly.

"Of course," I answered.

"Could you tell her that I love her?" He gently placed both of his hands on either side of my face, steadying me. His piercing hazel eyes steeled on mine. "I love you, Emma. The thought of losing you today, the reality of me not being there to protect you, it killed me. I may be your Guardian, but I need you just as much as you need me."

I was nearly breathless, my heart drummed loudly. "The girl, she just told me to tell you something."

"Yes?"

"She said...to kiss me already," I exhaled.

I raised my hand and captured the back of his neck again. His hungered mouth once again possessed mine. As our lips and mouths connected, I felt like I was floating.

Placing both hands under the back of his shirt, I gently felt his scars.

He flinched away from me.

"Do they hurt? Your scars?" I asked, concerned I'd hurt him.

"No."

"I want to feel them then," I whispered. He complied and I pulled up his shirt, moving around him to gently kiss his back. "Thank you for saving me that day. I'm so sorry you had to endure all this pain."

He turned around to face me and wrapped me in his arms.

"I told you, don't ever be sorry."

I leaned back in to kiss him again when I heard laughter echo down the hallway.

Oh crap.

Kade quickly gave me one last kiss, before he clicked on the light. I bent down to pick up my apple when Courtney and Lia appeared in the doorway.

"Well, no wonder you took so long. We thought you were lost," Lia laughed.

"Nope, I was just telling Kade goodnight," I said, glancing at him. His eyes shimmered as he grinned.

"We ran out of soda, and you can't have water with popcorn," Lia stated.

"That is very true," I agreed. "And not just any soda…"

"Dr. Pepper," we cheered in unison.

"That cupboard, second shelf," Courtney pointed.

Kade chuckled, so I turned to him with a grin. "Are you sure you don't wanna join us? It'll be an entire night of fun-fun-fun," I cheered oh-so enthusiastically.

Lia couldn't let this opportunity pass. "Come on, Kade. You have to come, or Emma will have her head in the clouds the whole night, wishing you were with her."

I glared at her.

"What? You know I'm right."

"She *has* been my best friend for the past three years. She does know me," I admitted.

"Damn, right. Hell, if I were in your place, Emma, I'd be wishing the same thing," she laughed. "Come on. Don't make me beg, Kade. It's not a pretty sight."

He blushed, and shook his head.

"Please?" I gazed at him with puppy dog eyes. "You can have my pillow."

"What will you use?" Courtney asked.

"She'll use this," Kade said, patting the spot, right between his arm and collar bone. I smiled. He was too perfect. He glanced at me and winked.

"Oh stop. You guys are killing me with cuteness," Lia huffed.

Courtney giggled, covering her mouth. Her cheeks flushed with bright pink.

"So are you coming, Kade?"

"I guess I have no choice. I'm outnumbered three-to-one."

"You really don't have to come, if you don't want to," I said.

"No, I want to," he answered, looking directly into my eyes. "Staying up all night, filling myself with crap, watching a movie with you…it all sounds amazing."

Even if I didn't get the same electrical shock, or the instant euphoric feeling I got when he was an immortal, with just a look, Kade still did a number on my emotions.

Either way, there was a bond which connected his heart to mine. He was everything good in the world, wrapped up into the most beautiful package, and sent to me. We were so different, yet connected. How could I have been so blessed?

We grabbed the drinks, a few more snacks, and headed back upstairs.

The movies played, but somewhere between the second and third, I fell asleep, safe and snug in Kade's arms.

EIGHTEEN

WHEN I WOKE, I WAS on Courtney's bed with a blanket pulled over me, and Kade was gone. My four companions were sprawled out all over the floor, and body parts were strewn in every direction amidst stray pieces of candy and popcorn.

I took my pillow and quietly tiptoed through the maze of bodies, trying to avoid stepping on anyone. When I finally made it safely to my bedroom, I pressed the pillow to my face and breathed in the sweet lingering scent. Even his smell brought a smile to my face. I placed it back on my bed and then headed over to the window, and pulled back the curtain.

It was the most beautiful day outside. The sun was shining, the sky was clear, and gentle breezes rustled the fresh new leaves on the trees.

As much as I wanted to see the beauty in everything around me, I couldn't. Not today. My head was shrouded in a dark cloud of sadness, and every cell within me was filled with gloom and pain.

Today was the day we were going to bury my parents.

This day was supposed to be part of a closure in my life that I wasn't ready or prepared for. My parents were my world. They instilled every good thing they possessed into me, and in an instant, they were gone. And I was never given chance to say goodbye.

There were no last loving words, no last hugs, and no last kisses. One moment they were sitting in the front seat of the car, laughing and singing along with the radio, and the next, their lifeless bodies were being crated to Alaska.

The day they were taken from me proved how very fragile and unpredictable life really was. I thought I was headed one way, only to have it tumble out of control, and then land in the completely opposite direction. My head had still not settled. Deep inside I wished to see my parents walk through the front door, take me by the hand, and lead me home to live out the rest of our happy, normal life.

But life was sometimes unkind, and didn't give second chances. Instead it gave you two choices. You could either curl up and die, or get up and try again.

Getting up takes huge amounts of effort. It means bearing down and pushing through the toughest of times, even if you have to create barriers around your heart, and grow an extra layer of skin. But it also gives you a strength you probably never knew you'd possessed. An ember begins to glow. The glow eventually sparks, breathing new flame, which fuels a hope and desire to live.

These were the things my parents taught me. Things I didn't care about, or ever gave a second thought about – not until I had to live it.

Within myself, I had made the decision to get up. But I was still trying to regain my balance. I could feel that tiny ember smoldering inside of me, but I knew if there was any hope of it sparking, it would come from the strength they instilled in me. They would never die. They would forever live on in my heart, my actions, and what I would someday pass on to my own children.

My best friends slept most of the day away, and when they woke, the atmosphere remained somber. Everyone seemed down today. We ate lunch, and then got ready.

It was late afternoon when we all made our way down a cobbled path leading to the cemetery. A violin started playing a beautiful song as we all gathered.

We were now outside of the protected barrier, so everyone except Alaine, Samuel, Kade, and my four mortal friends were out there watching, guarding, and protecting the area, making sure we were safe.

I had to explain Samuel's presence to Jeremy and Lia, since they hadn't seen him before. I told them he was Alaine's new love, and they immediately bought it. They were perfect together.

We stood in a small, open area. An intricate stone wall separated the cemetery from the outside. It was quiet and peaceful. The grass was soft and well-manicured. Outside of the wall towered spruce and birch trees which swayed back and forth to the peaceful sounds of the wind and violin. Bright multicolored tulips and wildflowers were beginning to bloom all around us.

Aside from all of this, you couldn't help but notice the two large holes excavated to hold the exquisite coffins.

On each of their coffins, Alaine placed a picture; a self-portrait of each of them.

My dad looked so handsome dressed in a black business suit and lavender tie. His hair was combed back, and his blue eyes sparkled just as brightly as his smile. He had the best smile, and the best laugh. Whenever he laughed, everyone around him followed, because he was that infectious.

The picture of my mother was taken at the beach. She was sitting on her chair. Her sun-kissed hair was pulled back from her perfect, porcelain face. Her lips and cheeks were a soft pink, and her eyes were big and bright green. Her face was beaming with love and laughter. This is how I remembered her best. She was the epitome of joy.

God, I missed them.

My eyes began to well up with hot tears and every cell in my body ached. They were so full of life, and had so much more to give. But they were murdered. Stolen away from me much too soon, and it wasn't fair.

"Are you okay?" Lia whispered, taking hold of my hand.

I nodded, trying to hold back the unavoidable tears, but they finally spilled over and rushed down my cheeks. I quickly wiped my face and turned to gather myself.

This is when I noticed two gravestones off to the left. One was

Alaine's late husband, and the other was Courtney and Caleb's mother. Caleb had just walked Courtney over to their mother's stone, each of them carrying freshly-cut, red roses. I watched as Caleb knelt, and dusted away a few leaves which had fallen around on her plot. He then gently placed his roses down.

Courtney leaned over and hugged her mother's stone, whispering something so silent, only she and her mother could hear. My heart ached and empathized with them. I watched Courtney wipe the tears falling from her red eyes. She finally knelt and placed her roses down next to Caleb's. He wrapped his arm around his sister, and they stood in silence, remembering.

Lia and Jeremy stood to the right of me, and Samuel and Alaine to the left. Kade came and stood directly behind me. I was glad he was there. He always had my back, and today I would need him there more than ever.

Alaine called a local minister to perform the ceremony. When he arrived, he took his spot at the front, and everyone went silent. He was a stout man, with wispy gray hair, greased and flattened to his scalp. He wore a black robe, and carried an aged Bible in his hand, with colored note cards sticking out from various pages.

The violinist changed songs and played softly as the minister opened his Bible and began the ceremony. His words offered faith, hope, and an assurance that my parents were in heaven, and that one day we would meet them again. I wished and hoped, with my entire being, that he was correct because his words offered me something I could hold onto. A life after death.

My body felt completely numb, and I wished my mind would be

too. The ceremony was a blur and before I knew it, it was almost over. The minister asked if I wanted to say something about my parents, but the thought of speaking about them sent a tidal wave of emotion crashing through me which was almost unbearable. Alaine grasped my hand, and assured me it was okay.

Jeremy and Lia cried through the entire ceremony, but I tried my best to hold on. I tried to remember the wonderful and happy times we shared. I tried to be strong because I knew they didn't want us to shed tears for them, but rather celebrate their life instead of death. They would want us to be filled with comfort, not grief.

As their caskets were being lowered into the ground, reality hit me like a brick. This was final. My parents were dead. Their lifeless bodies, shrouded behind those beautiful boxes, were about to be placed in the earth for all eternity.

Lia suddenly turned to Jeremy and buried her face into his shoulder, sobbing. He wrapped his arm around her as tears streamed down his own face.

Samuel held Alaine tightly in his arms, and I heard her soft cries.

I tried to be strong, but the veil of sorrow was wrapped too tightly around me. Blinded by despair, I ran forward to my mother's casket and threw myself over it. At that very moment, whatever was left of my broken heart, shattered into a million pieces.

I wept until my body was too weak to move, and then dropped to the cold ground between them.

This wasn't a dream. This was my nightmare.

Strong, protective arms suddenly wrapped around me, holding me tight.

Kade was always there to pick me up when I needed him most. He knew I was broken, and he came to hold me together. I turned toward him, and wrapped my arms around his neck, and cried. He sat on the ground with me, rocking, comforting, and cradling me in his arms.

"It will be alright," he whispered over and over again, never loosening his embrace. "Everything will be alright."

I knew I would eventually get through this, especially with him by my side.

He pressed his lips to my forehead and wiped my tears. "I'll always be here for you, Emma."

"I know you will," I sobbed.

"Please don't give up on me. On us," he whispered.

"I won't." I promised.

That was the second time he spoke those words, almost pleading for me not to give up on him. I wondered if he thought Ethon was more appealing because he was immortal and had wings. Although appealing, they weren't more appealing than what Kade had proven. His love and loyalty surpassed wings and speed.

Noticing I was pulling out of my unglued state of sadness, Lia and Jeremy slowly made their way over. Kade helped me up, and as soon as I stood, Lia and Jeremy wrapped their arms around me. In our huddle we all cried again. They knew my parents and spent a lot of time at our home. My parents loved them, and treated them like part of our family.

After we cried it out, I finally made my way over to Samuel and Alaine.

"Thank you so much for doing this. It was a beautiful ceremony, and I know my parents are happy to be resting here. There couldn't have been a more beautiful place."

"It was my pleasure, sweetheart," Alaine said, hugging me. "Victoria was my only sister. I loved her and Christian. We left our most precious treasure in their hands. That's how much we trusted and respected them. They deserved so much more."

Samuel and Alaine hugged me, and we stayed and watched as the last pieces of dirt covered the graves. Even though it felt like the walls were tumbling down around me, I would keep climbing because that's what they would have wanted.

Alaine covered the plots with the biggest, most beautiful bouquets of flowers. In between the graves she set a large carving of an Angel, much like the ones in the ballroom. He was beautiful, about eight feet tall. His face was solemn, his wings spread out behind his back, and his arms outstretched over each of my parent's graves. A perfect Guardian Angel, who would be watching over them in their eternal sleep.

I was glad to have my best friends here with me.

The three of us sat in the cemetery and talked and about the many memories we shared with my parents. Kade stood near the exit, waiting and watching, giving us our moment. When the sun finally started to set, and it felt right to leave, I said my final good-bye.

As we left the gate, Ethon was standing there, holding three red roses in his hand, which were almost the same color as his eyes.

"I'm sorry for your loss, Emma," he said stepping forward,

offering them to me. "The opened roses are for your parents, and the one that's still closed, is for you. With the love and support around you, it's just a matter of time before you bloom."

"Thank you," I said, holding them in my grasp. "They're beautiful."

"You're welcome," he answered. He glanced behind me and his eyes locked onto Kade. His eyes were blank, as he turned to leave.

"That's really sweet of you, Ethon," Lia said. His head twisted, he gave her a slight smile, and then walked away.

Lia wrapped her arm around me and led me toward the house.

Miss Lily made an amazing buffet dinner with many different types of yummy food, but I barely ate. My insides were still too sore.

After dinner, we went upstairs. When I opened the door to my room, Lia grabbed my arm.

"I'll be right back. I have something for you, but I left it in my room."

"Alright," I answered. Jeremy and I entered my room, and he plopped on my bed and dropped backward.

"Tomorrow is our last day here, can you believe it?" He asked. "It seems like we just got here. The days just flew by."

"I know. *Way* too fast," I sighed

"Well, we have to do something fun," he said.

My stomach twisted wondering what he could have wanted to do. "Yes, definitely," I said. "We will have to make tomorrow the best day ever." And it would have to be safe.

A wide grin formed on his face.

Lia knocked and entered. She walked over and handed me large, flat box. I pulled one of the sides open and pulled out a scrapbook.

"Wow, how did you get this?" I asked.

"I asked Alaine if she could pick one up for me, and I would pay her back. Of course she refused to take my money, but I thought it would be nice for you to have. You know, to put your memories in."

"Thank you, Lia," I said, wrapping my arms around her neck. She hugged me back.

I went to my closet and pulled out the box filled with hundreds of pictures. That night, the three of us sat and sorted through all of them.

My mom had written the date, my age, and the location of each picture.

I carefully traced my finger over her handwriting. She was so detailed and it made me smile. If I could be half the woman she was, I'd be happy.

NINETEEN

THIS WAS THE VERY LAST day I had with Jeremy and Lia, and I didn't want it to end with sadness. So, I pulled myself out of bed and decided there would be no more tears or glum faces.

None of them had a clue of what they wanted to do, so I thought I'd go and ask Alaine for suggestions. When I came down the stairs, she was on her way to her study, and waved me to follow her. It must have been something good, because she had a large smile on her face.

In her study she snapped the door shut behind us.

"Hey sweetheart, how are you doing today?" She asked.

"I'm great today. I've decided there will be no more tears while they are here."

She smiled at me and shook her head. "You are amazingly strong." She leaned forward and gave me a hug. "So, before I tell you my surprise, did you want to ask me something?"

"Yes, since today is their last day, I was wondering what we could do to make it memorable."

Her smile widened. "I thought it would be fun to have a going-away party for your friends in the ballroom tonight. I've already hired a DJ, and a decorator. I know its last minute, so we didn't have many options. I just told them to make it black and white."

"Oh, that's awesome," I squeaked. "This is going to be amazing, and black and white is pretty befitting." My life had once been clear-cut, black and white, but now, the colors had starting to bleed together into an ugly gray. That gray seemed to follow me everywhere. I just had to remember to keep finding the silver lining.

"Yes, and black and white coordinate with any color," she smiled.

"Do you think we could make it a Masquerade party? I've always wanted to go to one, but never had the chance," I asked, knowing it was a far-fetched idea, given the time.

"Yes, we can. I actually had a Masquerade Ball here last year, and still have a box full of masks stored somewhere in the attic. I also have a bunch of extra Victorian gowns from a theatre company which shut down a few years back. They are also in storage. I'll have James go and pull them out for me. There should be something in the box for you, Courtney, and Lia, but I'm afraid I don't have anything for Jeremy."

"Oh, that's okay. Jeremy won't wear anything but shorts and a button up shirt anyway. Thank you so much," I said, hugging her tightly. I was just about to leave, and then paused and turned back to her. "I also wanted to let you know I really can't thank you enough for all you've done for me. I could never imagine how hard it must have been for you to give me up, but I really had a wonderful life. And it was because you allowed me to."

"Oh, Emma," she said, stepping forward and cupping my face in her hands. "You don't know how much those words mean to me. Your safety was, and will always be, my main priority. I just hope I can offer you just as much happiness as they did." She leaned forward and kissed my cheek.

"Maybe, once this war is over and Lucian is gone," I said.

"Yes," she breathed. "We all hope it will end soon."

I hugged her and left. Running back up the stairs, I couldn't wait to tell Jeremy and Lia about the Masquerade Ball. As soon as it left my mouth, Lia grabbed me and swung me around in a circle, squealing. Jeremy wasn't too thrilled about it, until I told him he could wear whatever he wanted.

Then we went and made the announcement to Courtney and Caleb, who were thrilled that they would finally get to attend a party in the ballroom.

At least it kept us in the house, and kept them busy and excited.

James eventually pulled out the gowns from storage, but they were too musty smelling and badly wrinkled. Thankfully, Courtney had a back-up plan. Because she and Lia were almost the same size, she dragged her into her closet to look for dresses. Courtney had a whole row of beautiful dresses, which were perfect for a masquerade ball.

Just as I wondered what I was going to wear, there was a soft rapping on the door. When I opened it, James was standing there.

"Hello, Emma. I'm so sorry to bother you," he said, talking in a quieted voice.

"Hi James," I returned. "It's really nice to see you again."

"It's nice to see you as well," he smiled warmly.

"Please, come in," I said, stepping to the side.

He took one step inside the door and then handed me a long, black garment bag. The last time I'd seen one like this, it carried the magical super suit.

"Alaine, asked me to bring this to you. She said it's something for you to wear to the Ball tonight."

"Really?" I bubbled. Excitedly, I took it from his hands, my stomach twisting with anticipation.

"She said if you'd like something else, just let her know."

"No. I'm sure this will be perfect. Thank you so much."

He smiled, and then shut the door as he left.

I carried the bag to the closet and hung it up. My fingers tingled as I carefully zipped it open to reveal a simple, yet elegant white gown. It had spaghetti straps, with a sweetheart cut, and was fitted around the bust and waist with shimmering iridescent beads. From the waist down, the material was soft and flowed to the floor. In another pouch, I found elegant, white high heels in my size. How did she know?

With about three hours left before the party, I zipped it back up.

I could hear Courtney and Lia laughing and chatting away, trying on dresses a room down.

Jeremy was with Caleb in his room, playing some war video

game. The floor seemed to rumble and boom with sounds blaring from his surround sound.

It was their last day, and they were each having a wonderful time…without me. I knew it was inevitable, but I didn't think it would happen this fast. I wasn't the same girl who left LA a few months ago.

I yawned, still tired from the whole day before. I lay on my bed and decided to take a nap until they came back. Not too long after I rested my head on my pillow, I was out.

I stayed that way until I was rudely awakened by abrupt shaking. Lia and Courtney were jumping on the bed, trying to get me up.

"Wake up, sleepy-head. The party's in an hour. We have to start hair and makeup," Courtney beamed. She spent many hours on online, learning all the different makeup techniques.

"Can I just wear my hair back in a ponytail?" I asked.

"Emma. Are you kidding me? This is a Masquerade Ball, and there will be gorgeous guys all dressed up down there. You can't show up with a ponytail. Courtney will be your makeup artist, and I will be your hair designer. Now, off to the bathroom Cinderella, or you'll be late for the ball."

I dragged myself to the bathroom. Lia plugged in the flat and curling irons, while Courtney spread make-up all over the bathroom counter.

She closed the toilet lid. "Sit," she ordered.

"Yes, sir," I said in a military voice. She huffed and rolled her eyes.

I sat there for forty-five minutes while they had their way with me. They both took turns beautifying themselves in between trying to make me up. They looked beautiful.

Lia used a darker makeup for her eyes, and added false eyelashes. Her lips were painted with bright red lipstick, which looked amazing against her straight black hair and honey complexion.

Courtney's light brown hair fell in large ringlets down her shoulders. Her bright, blue eyes were framed with more natural colors, and dark mascara which made them stand out.

When they were done with me, they stood there with wide smiles, before turning to give each other high fives.

"I better not look like a prostitute," I said.

"If you did, you would be high-end. Like an escort," Lia said flatly. "Now we need to get you in that dress before we can give you the full reveal."

Courtney went to the closet and grabbed the black garment bag, and Lia hung it on the shower rod to unzip it.

"Wow, girl. You are totally going be Cinderella. Just make me a deal?" Lia asked.

"Sure, what is it?" My eyes narrowed on her.

"When you finally choose your Prince Charming, I want the castoffs. Or, I'll just take Dominic. He's really tall though. I think the top of my head hits his belly button, but that's okay. He can just pick me up and put me in his pocket. I'll be his munchkin."

Courtney looked at her with a deeply furrowed brow, and I burst into laughter.

"Sorry, Courtney. Sometimes she is just totally random," I said.

"Yeah, sorry. There are times when my mouth needs to be leashed," Lia added.

They helped me get into my gown and then slowly zipped it up.

"Oh. My. God." Lia had her hand over her mouth. "You seriously look like an angel."

"Are you ready to see our handiwork?" Courtney asked.

I took in a deep breath and nodded.

"Okay, close your eyes."

I shut my eyes and they led me out of the bathroom and into my closet, which had a full length mirror inside.

"Alright...open!" Courtney said.

I opened my eyes and froze. I didn't even recognize the girl staring back at me. She had been completely transformed.

The makeup was light and natural, with a slight shimmer to it. The natural colors highlighted all of my features. My eyelashes looked a lot longer with mascara and were perfectly curled up. My cheeks were lightly dusted in pink, and my lips were glossed in a rose color. The gown sparkled at the top and flowed perfectly to the bottom.

"So?" Lia asked.

I smiled, but was speechless.

"I think she likes it," Courtney said.

"No, think she loves it," Lia giggled.

"You guys are simply amazing, and you both look gorgeous," I said. "Thanks. I'm completely..."

"Speechless?" Courtney asked.

"Exactly," I said. I could feel my eyes begin to water.

"Oh no. Don't you dare, Emma Wise. You better suck those tears back into those ducts right now," Lia scolded.

I laughed and quickly pressed a Kleenex to the corner of my eyes.

They came and stood next to me. Lia wore a short black dress, which poofed out. Her black high heels were almost three inches tall.

Courtney also wore a shorter dress which flared out just above her knees. Hers was light pink, and had a big bow attached on the left side. Her heels were only an inch tall and were white.

We dug through the masks and found ones to match our wardrobe. Mine was a hand held Victorian mask, white with sparkles and white feathers on one side.

Lia had a black mask which covered the top half of her face, and Courtney actually found a pink and white one. The pink was darker than her dress, but it worked.

"Well, ladies. The party started five minutes ago. What do you say we make our entrance," Lia said.

"Let's!" Courtney cheered.

They both left ahead of me, so I stepped out and closed the door behind us.

They squealed and excitedly ran down the hall. I heard Courtney yell, "Don't start the party without us!" Laughter echoed upward from the bottom of the stairs, followed by whistles and catcalls.

"You ladies look beautiful," Dominic said.

Lia turned to me as she was heading down the stairs and squealed. "Hurry up, Emma. And, don't forget your mask," she whispered loudly.

I wanted to go back in the room and hide, but I sucked in a deep breath and walked forward. At least I could hide behind the mask. As I made it to the end of the hall, I lifted the mask to my face. When I reached the top of the stairs, all of the Guardians were at the bottom, along with Alaine. They were all facing the stairwell, looking at me silent - like stones.

Was something wrong?

I suddenly felt naked and wanted to run back into my room and hide. Then Kade pushed forward, from behind Thomas and Alexander.

My heart instantly swooned and then quickly picked up pace as he stepped to the bottom stair.

He was wearing an all-white tuxedo, with matching shoes. His hair was neatly combed back, and his face illuminated like an angel. His dreamy hazel eyes gleamed as they fixed on to me. The way he smiled, melted me to my core. Every step I took closer to him made my body tingle in anticipation of his touch.

As I focused on him, it was as if he and I were the only ones in the room.

"Hey, Emma," Dominic called, breaking my concentration. I glanced up. He was wearing a black tuxedo with golden accents, and a golden mask covering the top half of his face. His hair was neatly brushed back, and he was holding up thumb. "You look ravishing."

"Thanks," I blushed. "Courtney and Lia created me."

"Yes, we did," Courtney said loudly.

"She's looks stunning," Alaine said. "You ladies did an amazing job, and you both look beautiful as well."

"Thank you," they answered.

Music started to play and echoed down the hallway.

"Shall we?" Alaine announced, and winked at me as she started towards the ballroom. James escorted her, and I was wondering why Samuel wasn't here. Maybe the protective barrier was still around the house, so he couldn't enter. That wasn't very fair. Alaine was exquisite, and carried herself with a stylish grace. He should be able to see her all dressed up.

"Shall we?" Dominic offered his arm to Lia. She froze, and then her head snapped to me. Her eyes were filled with an expression of shock and excitement. I smiled and nodded at her. She turned back to Dominic and linked her arm under his. Her face was lit up like the sun, and I knew he had just made her entire night.

"Thank you," I mouthed to him. He gave me a wink in return.

Jeremy, dressed in long, black shorts and a black button-down dress shirt, walked up to Courtney and held his arm out. She grinned and took it, and they proceeded down the hall, followed by the remaining guests.

All except Kade.

My gaze focused back on his luminous face. At this moment, I was in a fairy tale, and he was my Prince Charming.

As I came down the stairs, he held out his hand to me. The pleasured look in his eyes pulled at my heartstrings. I placed my hand in his and he gently led me down the last stair, into his personal space.

He softly ran his palms over the exposed skin on my shoulders and down the length of my arms, until he captured my hands in his. I trembled against his touch, as electricity sparked through every cell.

He leaned forward, his heated breath tickled against my neck.

"You're so beautiful," he whispered. The warmth in his voice settled my tensed body.

"Thank you," I breathed. Whenever he was this close, my mind went into a fog. "And you look amazing."

A smile edged at the corners of his sculpted mouth.

"I want to kiss you, but I'm afraid it will ruin your lipstick."

"I can always go back up and apply more."

"No. We have all night," he said, with a playful gleam in his eyes. "Besides, I don't know if that shade of red is my color."

We both laughed.

"Alright then. I'll take a rain-check."

"And I'll be more than happy to redeem it," he grinned. "Shall we?" He held his arm out to me.

"Definitely," I answered. Butterflies swirled inside of me as I hooked my arm through his.

TWENTY

E LED ME DOWN THE hall into the Ball Room. I was overwhelmed at the beauty of this place. The transformation was unbelievably gorgeous. Sheer elegance.

The large chandelier above us emitted a warm glow, sparkling off its teardrop crystals. The sconces along the walls were another source of warm lighting. Around the room, statues of Angels were up-lit, making them stand out. Crystal vases were set on smaller pedestals, carrying large bouquets of white flowers.

The DJ set up his booth in the corner. He dressed according to the theme, and wore a black mask, and a black and red cape. He had placed laser lights and speakers around the floor.

On the opposite side of the room were four round dining tables. White linen, fine china, crystal glasses, silver utensils, and the most gorgeous white floral centerpieces adorned the tabletops. There were two servers standing by, their arms folded over their chests, talking to each other.

Everyone started heading toward the tables to sit down.

The DJ suddenly changed the music and put on a slow song.

Kade stopped, then turned to me and bowed. "Emma Wise, may I have this first dance?"

"Right now?" I asked.

"Of course," he said, holding his hand out to me.

I smiled and stepped forward, resting my hands on his strong shoulders. His arms encircled my waist, drawing me closer. I settled my head on his chest, while his sweet aroma enveloped me.

He and I were floating on a dream. The song, the man, the love we shared...it all spoke directly to me, and couldn't have been more perfect. Kade was my everything.

He had loved me back to life, from the moment we met. His love and presence were my stability when the world became unbalanced. He had protected me, selflessly gave up his immortality, and now offered his mortal life for me.

There were two silver linings to Kade's mortality. Not only would my love get to stay with me when the time came for the Guardians to go back to Midway, but his mortality also proved something. It established that our love, our strong connection, was fortified on more than a magical bond. I was not mindlessly in love, or made to feel attracted to him because of some supernatural forces. What Kade and I shared was real. I had a choice in the matter, and I willfully chose him.

Tears threaten my eyes, but I fought them. I knew I was the

luckiest girl in the world. I was so blessed to have such a selfless, loving life in my arms.

I hugged him tighter and he smiled against my cheek.

We danced until the song was over, and then I stepped back and gazed into his eyes.

"Thank you," I breathed.

"For what?"

"For loving me."

His eyes softened. "It's easier than breathing."

"Get a room you two!" Dominic yelled from across the room. We both turned to him, and I blushed. Everyone was laughing, except Alaine. She shot Dominic a look of cease-and-desist.

I was so lost in the moment, I'd forgotten the room was filled with everyone else. Lia's smile was as bright as a beacon, and the largest I'd seen yet. I could tell she was happy for me. She liked Kade from the moment she met him.

Taking me by the hand, he led me to the tables, pulled out my chair, and then sat down next to me. Lia, Jeremy, Caleb, and Courtney were also seated around our table.

"Oh my God. You two looked so magical out there in white. Seriously. You both look angelic," Lia said. "It's really not fair."

I smiled. If she only knew.

"And, Emma, just at this place. It's beyond amazing…like royalty amazing. I can't believe she did all of this for Jeremy and me."

"I can. She's a very generous person," I said.

"She must really love angels. Those statues are breathtaking."

"Yes, she does have a thing for them."

"Well, your aunt must have had quite an inheritance."

"Her late husband was a doctor."

"Figures," she said. "And she invited all the neighbors. Do they not have girlfriends or wives?"

"Apparently not," I replied.

She shook her head in disbelief. "I have officially deemed this place the location of all gorgeous people. You better tell your Aunt to keep a room open because I'm totally moving in. Well, maybe after college, and after I find a job," she laughed. Pulling out her cell phone, she waved it around. "There may not be service, but I can still use the camera."

Lia made everyone lean in for a quick picture, and then proceeded to other tables on a picture binge. She even went and snapped a shot of the DJ, who gave her a wild pose.

Before dinner was served, I watched Alaine stand and whisper to the rest of the group, before walking out. *That was a bit odd.*

I looked at Kade, and he leaned over to whisper, "Samuel is coming. She went to get him."

I nodded, happy that he would be joining the event. It was only fair for him to get the chance to dance with Alaine.

But that also meant the protective barrier would come down. It was no wonder she alerted the other Guardians.

Our table continued to chat away, while the DJ played soft background music.

Caleb asked Lia if she wanted to dance after dinner, and she happily agreed. Jeremy also drummed up the nerve to ask Courtney, making her blush as she accepted.

I was glad to see smiles and laughter from my two best friends on their last night here. I hated to see them go. They had been such a bright light in my new world. I had laughed more in the past four days than I had during my entire stay.

Tomorrow would be bitter-sweet. I hated saying goodbye, but also felt a little better knowing we could still keep in touch via email or phone. This time I would be better at replying. If I wasn't dead.

After a few minutes, Samuel came walking in with Alaine on his arm. He looked so handsome. He was clean shaven, and wore a black suit with a silver tie.

Lia grabbed my arm and pulled me to her. "Your aunt's boyfriend is gorgeous. And you know what's super weird?" Her brow furrowed.

"What?" I asked.

"They could totally pass as your parents. You and Alaine look a lot alike, and oddly enough, you have his eyes." Her brow furrowed. Then her eyes steeled on mine, and shot back to Samuel. She closed her eyes and shook her head. "Weird."

"I kind of agree with you, Lia." I smirked at her mightily accurate observation.

They were perfect together, and possessed a love that was completely transparent. Two beautiful hearts forever bonded, and it exuded from every pore.

Samuel walked over after greeting everyone, and leaned down to whisper in my ear, "You look beautiful."

"Thank you," I said. "Lia, my friend over here, was just saying I have your eyes, and that I could pass as your daughter."

"Well, you are very sweet, Lia," Samuel said, turning to her. "Having Emma as a daughter would bring me nothing but happiness." Lia held her hand to her heart and looked like she might faint. She was such a drama queen.

He continued, "It was nice to meet both of you. I'm sad I didn't get a chance to know you better, but with circumstances as they are, it's been hard to make it here."

"Oh, it's totally understandable. It was nice meeting you," Lia said. Jeremy agreed.

Samuel turned to Kade with a nod, and then went to sit next to Alaine.

✦

After dinner the tables were cleared, and a punch and snack table were set up.

The DJ wasted no time, starting the night with some dance music.

"Since its Jeremy and Lia's last night here, let's say we get this party started!" He screamed into the microphone. All the lights went off, and were replaced by the DJ's laser lights around the dance floor.

The music was blaring so loud it reverberated right through, me throwing off the rhythm of my heart.

Everyone cheered.

When I turned to my friends, Lia was jumping up and down, clapping with the biggest smile on her face. Jeremy also wore a smile, but was a bit more reserved.

The four of them ran out to the dance floor.

"I think you owe me a dance," Dominic said, startling me.

I turned and he was bent over in a half-bow, with his hand held out to me. I smiled and took his hand. He tugged me out toward the others. Lia glared at me, with jealous eyes. I shrugged, and then she smiled and kept dancing.

We danced more than one song, but Lia and Courtney kept me there. Kade was sitting on the side, talking with the others. The DJ went to a slow song and Courtney and Lia wrapped their arms around Jeremy and Caleb.

Dominic leaned in, "I am going to get something to drink, but thanks for the dance. We're even now."

"No problem," I laughed.

As we left the dance floor, I felt a warmth and electricity rush through me. I turned to see two crimson eyes stepping out of the dark. Within a few strides, Ethon stood in front of me.

"Good evening, Emma," he said. He was dressed in a black tuxedo with crimson bow-tie and cummerbund. "Your beauty is breathtaking."

"Thank you," I said. "You look very dashing."

He smiled.

"I don't dance, but I am fairly good at swaying. Will you sway with me?" he asked.

I looked back to where Kade was sitting.

"Do you need his permission?" His voice sounded a bit irritated.

"No."

"Do you not want to dance with me?"

"Yes, I want to," I said.

I followed him out to the dance floor. As soon as Lia saw me with him, her jaw almost hit the floor. Jeremy also shot me a scrutinizing look.

Ethon turned to face me and gave me his hand. I took it and he pulled me in, the zap almost knocked me to my knees.

Lia and Jeremy's eyes never left me, and little did they know, I was dancing with the son of the Devil. I wondered what everyone else must have been thinking, seeing Ethon's arms wrapped around me so tightly.

But the bond was also wrapping around me, like a magnet drawing us closer. Our touch connected us even more than before. I could feel it. His crimson eyes burned bright. I tried to fight the pull, but it was so overwhelmingly strong. I tried to keep levelheaded, but all it did was make it ache.

"You're contacts glow in the dark?" Jeremy asked Ethon.

Ethon turned to him. "Yes. They are limited edition," he answered.

"Whoa, that is so awesome." Jeremy was captured by Ethon. At least I wasn't the only one.

He grabbed my right hand, lifted my arm, and swirled me around. Then led me around the ballroom.

My mind was in a haze and I was quickly becoming bewitched by him. My feet felt as if they were floating off the floor, and the world around us began to melt away. Ethon's seductive eyes narrowed onto mine and a grin crept up on his lips.

Bending down, my dark prince whispered, "You don't know

how much I want to take you away from here." His warm breath stimulated my neck, increasing my pulse.

"Where would we go?" I asked.

"Anywhere you want." Ethon pulled back to make eye contact.

My body instinctively tilted after him as he moved back. "How would we get there?"

"I'd fly, of course. I don't drive," he smiled coyly.

"I like flying," I answered.

He leaned forward, closing the gap. The buzz of the bond swirled around us, making me dizzy. "I know you do," he whispered between light kisses to my forehead and nose.

"Could I cut in?" A deep voice interrupted. Ethon's head snapped up and his fiery eyes burned, looking as if they would burn a hole right through Malachi.

"We're not finished," Ethon said.

"Well, this is my favorite song," Malachi answered.

Ethon glanced at me with distress painted in his fiery eyes, but he unwillingly handed me over. As soon as we disconnected, my body relaxed, and I fell into Malachi's arms. Ethon went off to the side and melded into the black background.

"Thank you," I whispered.

"No problem. I didn't want Kade to come and make a scene, so I figured I'd cut in."

"Ah, so you're the friend coming to the rescue. I thought you really wanted to dance with me," I teased.

"I don't dance," he answered flatly.

"Well you can sway, can't you?" I giggled.

"Maybe," he said. His brow had a constant furrow.

"Then will you sway with me for the remainder of this song? You *did* say it was your favorite." I grinned because I knew it wasn't. It was hilarious hearing this big, brawny guy say a romantic slow song was his favorite.

He shook his head. Malachi was wearing black slacks and a dark blue dress shirt. It looked like it had to be tailored because his shoulders were so broad. I placed my hands on his shoulders, and he placed his hands on my waist. He was stiff as a board.

"Just relax, and rock back and forth. Like this."

His face was hard with concentration.

"You've got it," I praised. Having fun yet?"

"No," he snarled. I could tell he felt awkward, and his eyes never left our feet.

"Well, the song is almost over."

"Good."

As soon as the song ended, Malachi disconnected from me. Upbeat dance music started blaring and I could tell that was where he drew the line.

"Thanks," Malachi mumbled and walked off. As he exited, Alexander entered.

"Hey, Emma. Want to dance?" He asked with a wide smile on his face.

"Sure."

We headed out to the floor and everyone was already jumping around and clapping. Who better to dance it with, than Alexander?

He was so full of energy, and this Guardian could actually dance.

He twisted and turned, and dropped in a half split and then easily slid back up. In between all of that, he performed some crazy foot movements. He must have done this before because I just stood in awe and clapped.

Courtney and Lia screamed and threw their arms in the air whenever he did something extra exciting. Even Caleb and Jeremy were smiling and clapping along. As the song reached the end, I saw Thomas slowly making his way out.

I guess I would be dancing with all of them. But that was more than fine with me. They were like my brothers. Besides, there was no one else they could dance with. Courtney and Lia were just having fun with Jeremy and Caleb, in their own little world.

"Thank you, Emma," Alexander said with a slight bow before exiting. It was like he hadn't even broken a sweat.

"That was all you, Alex," I laughed. "Thank you. You were awesome." He gave me a small salute and then jogged off.

Thomas was wearing black slacks and a white undershirt. He must have ditched the dress-shirt. His bleach blonde hair was a bit disheveled and his blue eyes were sparkling like the chandelier crystals.

"Let's dance," I said.

"I thought you'd never ask," he grinned.

He grabbed my hand and swirled me. He wasn't the greatest dancer, but he was jumping around like he thought he was, and it made me giggle. Courtney and Lia were laughing too. He actually didn't need me. Thomas was dancing in his own little world.

The song finally ended, and the DJ came back on. "Let's slow it down a bit and give everyone a chance to breathe."

"Thank you, Emma," Thomas said. He was breathing a little harder than Alexander, but he was also over a century older.

"So who put you all up to the dancing?" I questioned.

"Well, Kade suggested we all dance with you now because he's calling dibs on the last dance."

"Oh did he?" I chimed.

That was so sweet. I tried to find Kade, but everything beyond the dance floor, was pitch black. The laser lights made it even harder to see.

All four of my friends looked at each other and shook their heads. "We're gonna get something to drink," Lia said. "Are you coming?"

"Yes," I answered. As Thomas and I walked off the dance floor, Samuel and Alaine walked on, hand in hand, their eyes were fixed on each other. Lucky in love.

Tony Bennett's, *The Way You Look Tonight* started playing.

When they took center stage, Samuel clasped Alaine's left hand in his right, and then placed his other on her shoulder. She stood with perfect posture, and then they started to move. Slowly and gracefully, he led her in a slow waltz around the ballroom. It was one of the most breathtaking things I had ever witnessed. They were floating effortlessly across the floor. Their gazes were steeled on each other, and filled with so much passion and emotion, it instantly warmed me.

They were everything I wanted and hoped for my future to be. The thought sent a sudden rush of emotion through me, making my eyes water.

When they were done, everyone clapped and the DJ resumed his songs. The fantastic four found their way back out onto the dance floor. Thomas, Alexander, and Dominic made their way out to the floor as well, and had fun showing each other up, doing back flips and handsprings across the dance floor. They looked like they were having a blast, and I found myself with a large smile plastered to my face as I watched them.

I walked off to find Kade and spotted his silhouette standing against the back wall. He'd taken his jacket off, unbuttoned a few top buttons of his shirt, and rolled up his sleeves midway on his forearm. My heart tumbled inside as I made my way over.

"You don't want to dance?" Kade asked as I drew close.

"Maybe later. My feet hurt. I'm going to give them a rest."

"Why don't you take your heels off?" he asked.

"Because this beautiful dress will drag all over the floor and get dirty. I'm fine. It's a common girl problem. I'll just rest a bit."

He suddenly grabbed me and pulled me up into his arms, cradling me.

I gasped at his suddenness. "What are you doing?"

"Sweeping you off of your feet," he chimed.

"You certainly have…you're becoming quite good at it."

A wave of déjà vu hit. I closed my eyes and remembered back in the cave, when my life was threatened by hypothermia. It was Kade's touch which brought me back to life. And then, he carried me in his protective arms, until I was strong enough to walk on my own.

"Practice makes perfect." He leaned down and gently pressed

his lips to my forehead. I closed my eyes and basked in his tenderness.

He was just so handsome. So magnetic. So completely perfect.

After a few songs played, he finally let me down. I glanced to my left and saw crimson eyes glowing in the darkness, and a wave of distressed emotion shot through my being.

Another slow song started playing.

"Would you like to dance?" Kade asked.

"Of course," I smiled. He led me to the dance floor with my hand in his.

I closed my eyes, shutting out the rest of the world - especially those red eyes haunting me from the darkness. I knew he was waiting for the right time to come to me. He wanted to hold me in his arms again, and I knew this because I could feel it.

TWENTY
ONE

I HATED THIS TUG OF war between hearts. I hated the bond - it thickened the air around me, suffocating me. When left on my own, I knew what I wanted. But the bond was merciless. It clouded all reason. I didn't need it. And I certainly didn't want it. I wanted to be in charge, even if I made the wrong decision.

I held tight to Kade. This was our moment in time together, and I wanted it to last. We swayed in each other's arms, and it felt perfect.

After the song was finished, I knew Ethon was closing in. I could feel him. I opened my eyes and he was standing right beside us.

Kade stepped in front of me. "What do you want?"

"You know exactly what I want. The bond cannot be controlled. I feel her emotions and I know exactly what she wants. Right now…it's not you," he sneered.

I stepped forward. "Stop it, Ethon," I rebuked.

"If you choose to be with him, you'll die," Ethon warned.

Kade stepped forward and faced off with him. "I would *die* for her."

"Yeah, much too easily," he scoffed.

"Are you threatening me?"

Ethon laughed in his face. "I don't threaten," his eyes went wicked.

The rest of the Guardians immediately surrounded us.

"You have no idea who you're up against, mortal. I could take you all out in one swipe…and therein lies the problem. If you loved her as much as you say you do, then you agree she's safer with me. It's just that simple. I can protect her. You cannot," Ethon taunted.

"You better put out that flame before it explodes," Dominic said, stepping up next to Kade.

"There will be no fighting here," Samuel said, coming in between them.

Ethon put his hands up and stepped back. "I only came to dance with Emma, like everyone else here has had the chance to do. Nothing more. They are the ones creating the monster."

"You keep your hands off of her, demon boy," Kade said.

"You know that's impossible," he grinned, teasing.

Kade suddenly sucker punched Ethon in the face. Ethon grabbed him by the neck and lifted him off the ground.

"Ethon, stop!" I screamed.

Dominic and Samuel rushed forward.

"Step back, or I'll crush him," Ethon threatened.

"Try it," Dominic matched his threat. "You harm him and they'll be wiping up pieces of you for the next decade."

"Ethon, don't," Samuel said in a calm voice. Ethon's eyes softened as he looked to Samuel. I could tell he respected him, but when Malachi stepped forward, his eyes went back to wicked.

I took a step closer to him. "Ethon. Leave him alone. Please." I begged. I knew the only way to calm his fire was to touch him. The bond had a way of quenching his fire. It worked before, hopefully it would work again.

I lifted my hand and placed it on the side of his face. Electricity buzzed through me and his eyes immediately shifted. I had captured them.

"Please," I whispered.

He dropped Kade and then turned to me. Dominic helped him to his feet.

"You have so much potential, Emma." Ethon said, sadly. "I only want what's best for you. Since we were bonded, that's all I've ever wanted."

I closed my eyes and shook my head, completely disconcerted.

"Just tell me. Right now, what do you want?" Ethon asked.

As much as it killed me inside, I fought and pushed the words out. "I need you to leave for now." As soon as I spoke the words my heart felt as if it had been pierced. I had a glimpse of what Ethon was feeling, and it made me sick inside. But I also knew that if he stayed, someone could get hurt. Someone could die.

"I'll leave, for you. Although, I know it's not truly what you want," he stated.

"I'll go with you," Samuel said. He nodded to Alaine, and her face saddened.

"Please tell your friends it was a pleasure meeting them," Ethon said.

Samuel glanced at me. "I'll see you in the morning."

I nodded.

Samuel laid his hand on Ethon's shoulder and led him out. Alaine followed after them.

Lia finally ran up to us.

She grabbed hold of my arm. "Did we miss something?"

"No. Ethon and Samuel had to leave. They were saying goodbye. Ethon said to tell you guys that it was a pleasure."

"Oh, bummer. I forgot to ask him where he ordered his contacts."

"I'll try and find out for you," I said.

Caleb came up next to Lia and she grabbed his hand. I looked at her and she wiggled her eyebrows. I smiled.

"The two of you hook up the night before you leave?" I rolled my eyes.

"Hey, better late than never. Plus, it seals the deal that I'm bringing my butt back here. Or, you can come to LA and spend some quality time with me."

"Definitely," I said, knowing full well that wasn't going to happen anytime soon.

Another fast song started pounding through the speakers.

"Want to dance?" Caleb asked her.

A wide smile crossed her face, and she glanced at me.

"Wanna come?"

"No thanks. Cinderella is about to lose her heels," I said. "Where's Jeremy?"

"Having some lengthy conversation with Courtney at one of the tables. *Boring*. She seemed interested, but I've learned to just walk away." She smiled and winked. "Later gator."

"Later," I laughed.

"Damn it. I was about to kick some ass," Dominic exhaled.

"Settle down," Malachi urged. "Go get some punch and a cookie."

They walked away, leaving me and Kade alone.

"I'm sorry, Emma," Kade said softly. "I shouldn't have hit him. It was pure instinct. I just couldn't help myself. This mortal body is so different. I have less control over my emotions, and it's so damn fragile."

"Don't be sorry. It was bound to happen," I said. "Are you alright?" I touched his neck.

"I'm fine. The downfall to being mortal is that I can't compete with his strength, and that freaking sucks."

"I'm sorry," I said sadly.

He shook his head. "What bothers me most is, he was right. Being mortal means I won't be able to protect you from the Fallen as I should. If you get hurt, it would crush me."

"You're mortal now, and I'm safe and sound," I stated.

His brow furrowed in anguish. "Yeah, thanks to Ethon...three times now."

I couldn't let this go on.

"Sometimes we let the worries of life overwhelm us so much that we forget to live. Let's just make each moment together the best we could ever imagine."

His eyes smiled at me. "You are wise beyond your years, Emma *Wise.*"

I rolled my eyes at his corny pun. "My parents taught me well."

"They would be so proud of you," he said, brushing his fingers over my cheek.

Alaine walked back into the room. "Kade, are you alright?"

He nodded.

"Emma, could I speak to you for just a minute?" she asked.

"Sure," I said. "Don't go anywhere. I'll be right back."

Alaine and I walked over to the snack tables.

"I thought it was better to have your friends fly out from Fairbanks tomorrow morning. It's less than an hour away, where Anchorage is hours."

"That's understandable."

"The only downfall is, you won't be able to see them off. It's too huge of a risk."

"Will they be safe?" I asked. That's all I needed to know. If they would be safe, then I would have no problem letting them go.

"Yes. They are in no threat. I'll send Courtney and Caleb with them, and Malachi and Dominic will also be going. I'm so sorry, but I just don't want to take any more risks with you."

"It's alright. I know they'll appreciate the fact they won't have to get up early to make the long drive. I just don't know what I'll tell them."

"I've already got that covered. I'll tell them you will have a

212

mandatory testing for advanced placement," she said.

"That'll work," I agreed. "They definitely won't question that, especially if it comes from you."

"Good. It's been arranged. I'll go speak to Jeremy now," she said.

"What time will they be leaving?"

"Their flight is at noon, so they will have to leave here by ten o'clock."

"Alright, thank you." My heart sank.

They would be leaving first thing in the morning, and the realization was crushing.

After Samuel and Ethon left, the party started to dissolve. I felt horrible the way it ended. I just couldn't handle my bonded in the same room. They were like oil and water. Or maybe more like vinegar and baking soda.

Caleb and Lia looked happy tonight. Both of them gleaming with first love syndrome. Their faces were glowing, plastered with permanent smiles, their hands never separating. They were adorable.

Courtney was also taken with Jeremy. But I wasn't sure if it was puppy love, or she was just amazed at how smart he was. She sat and listened to him, completely enthralled, which put him in his element. He had so much knowledge to share, and whenever he had the chance to share it, he was at his happiest.

The DJ finally called for the last dance.

"Jeremy and Emma! Get your booty's out here!" Lia yelled.

I glanced at Kade and he smiled. "I never thought you'd ask."

He led me to the dance floor, just as Jeremy walked Courtney out. I looked at my best friends. Our eyes all connected, and without a word, I knew this was our happiest moment. The three of us had been through a lot over the past three years. They had been my constant support, and now, they were here.

"Love you, girl," Lia said, holding her pinky out to me.

"Love you back," I replied, wrapping my pinky around hers. We would always be connected. She was my soul sister.

"And we love you too, Jeremy," she smiled.

"Yes, we do," I agreed.

Jeremy smiled, and pushed his glasses back on his nose. "The two of you irritate the hell out of me, but the feeling is mutual."

Courtney wrapped her arms around Jeremy's neck, and they both smiled at each other.

I held onto Kade and melted into his protective arms. This moment was magic. I wished I could press the freeze button and make it last. But time waits for no man. Mortal or immortal.

TWENTY TWO

AFTER THE DANCE, ALL THE rest of the Guardians left. The DJ quickly broke down his gear and had everything on his hand-cart in record time. I could tell he'd done this a lot.

Alaine came and said goodnight before she snuck into her room.

The six of us remained, and slowly made our way down the hall and up the stairway.

"So what do you guys want to do tonight?" I asked.

"Hang out with all of you until the sun comes up," Lia said.

"Another all-nighter?" I asked.

"It's what we do best," she replied throwing her arm around me.

"Yes, I know," I said. "So whose room will we be raiding tonight?"

"Yours. No television. Tonight it's all about us," she replied.

"Fine," I said.

When we reached the second level, Kade stopped.

"I think I'll be sitting this one out."

I turned and gave him a hug.

"Thank you for everything. I'll be seeing you tomorrow." He knew I needed some time alone with my friends.

"Goodnight everyone," he waved. "I'll see you all in the morning."

"Goodnight Kade," Lia chimed, and then the rest echoed.

Courtney, Caleb, and Jeremy went to their rooms, except for Lia. She stayed with me.

As we slipped in the room, I remembered something. "Hold on. I'll be right back," I told her.

"Go," Lia urged.

I quickly dashed back down the stairs and saw Kade just entering his room.

"Wait!" I called after him.

He paused and turned back to me.

"I've got a rain check that hasn't been redeemed, and I heard it expires at midnight."

His eyes narrowed and a crooked grin adorned his face. "I can definitely take care of that," he said.

I ran straight into his arms, and without hesitation and his beautiful mouth came down on mine, immediately taking possession. It was deep and passionate, and made the world around me spin. This was the perfect ending to this perfect night with him. When he pulled back, he had a smile cemented on his face.

"That was some redemption," I breathed, my head still spinning.

He laughed and gave me three last kisses before releasing me. "Goodnight Miss Wise."

"Goodnight, Mr. Anders."

He bowed his head, and gave me one last smile before ducking into his room.

I stumbled back to my room, dizzy, with a silly smile plastered to my face. Lia was lying on my bed.

"Uh-oh, someone's love drunk," she laughed. "Girl, I know how you feel. He just steps near me and my world spins. You're so lucky. He looks as much in love with you as you are with him."

"How would you know?"

"I'm your best friend. I know things." She answered. "Plus, it's so damn obvious. You two were meant for each other. My beautiful bestie finally found her Prince Charming. And there are no bitches and ho's out here in the boonies to swipe him away. You are totally lucky." We both burst into laughter. She stood up and straightened out her dress.

"Thank you for coming, Lia. I really needed you here."

"Hey, that's what friends are for." She hugged me. "Now go get changed. The night is young!" she said, lifting her arm in the air as she walked out the door.

I made my way to the bathroom and slipped out of my gown, turning the page on this beautiful fairy tale moment. I wished I could have edited out the drama, but that was part of my never-ending adventure. I glanced at myself one last time, before washing away the remnants of the evening.

Somewhere during the beginning of the night I'd lost my mask, but I was already hiding behind my own mask.

I wished I could tell my friends my secret, but the risk was too great. If they breathed a word, or if the immortals found out, they would be in real danger.

If they ever found out, I knew they'd understand - well, maybe not at first. Let's be serious. They would freak. After the initial shock wore off, Lia would probably hug me, and Jeremy would definitely ask a million questions of which I had no answers.

I smiled at the glimpse of what could have been.

About an hour later, the gang returned in their sleeping clothes with pillows. Courtney and Lia had raided the kitchen again for more snacks and drinks, which were put in the middle of the floor. Then, we sat in a circle and reminisced about our years together. The first time we met in the cafeteria. The countless sleepovers. The school dances we went stag to, and ended up dancing with ourselves and going home alone. Beach outings, picnics in the back yard, long study nights, close calls behind the wheel, weekend mall outings, movie marathon nights, and countless pillow fights.

The good, the bad, and the ugly. They were there. We were, and would always be, the Three Musketeers.

Courtney and Caleb shared a little about their years here, but they seemed more interested in our stories. Lia was the best at telling them. She was so animated, and made us all laugh.

In between stories, we played board games and cards. And a few hours before the sun came up, they all fell sound asleep. But my mind couldn't rest. I smiled at the peaceful faces of my friends. In just a few short hours, they would be gone. At least I still had Courtney and

Caleb to keep me grounded.

I stood by the window, pulled back the curtain, and watched the darkened sky slowly begin to wake. I was mesmerized, watching the stars disappear, only to be replaced with a soft golden glow. Before long, brilliant shimmering rays spread above the mountain in the backdrop, illuminating our little spot in the world. It was breathtaking.

I closed my eyes. My pale skin was thirsty, drinking up the warm, liquid gold pouring through the window. It was strange how comforting the sun was. It felt like a warm hug, offering a new day filled with hope. A new page. A new story. A new adventure.

After only a few hours of sleep, the alarm blared loudly, making me jump. Jeremy and Courtney shot up, but Lia and Caleb didn't budge. I swear I could even hear Lia snoring.

I walked over and clicked the alarm off. Now came the impossible task of waking Lia. She was not a morning person, to put it nicely. I could set off dynamite around her and she'd probably turn her head and fall back to sleep.

"I'm going to get ready," Courtney said. She was still half-asleep when she dragged her pillow and her feet out the door.

Jeremy stretched, put on his glasses, and made his way to the bathroom. In a few minutes, he returned with a small cup filled with cold water. He was more than familiar with the risk he was taking, but it was usually the only way. She hated it, and he was in jeopardy of sustaining an injury.

"Lia, if you don't get up, I'm going to dump water on your face," he loudly teased. She didn't budge. "Second warning. Ice water *will* be applied to all sleeping persons."

Caleb suddenly sat up. His hair was sticking up on one side, and pressed flat on the other.

"Good morning, sleepy head," I giggled.

"Morning," his voice cracked.

He glanced at Lia, and then up to Jeremy who was threatening her with the tilted glass.

"Wait. Let me leave first," Caleb said, pulling himself up. "I don't want to be here for this."

"Good idea," I said.

Caleb quickly stumbled out of the room.

"Lia!" Jeremy yelled. "Last chance. I've given you ample warning. You have three seconds!"

Lia snorted and started snoring again. I started laughing. "She hasn't heard your threats. Jeremy, you are totally playing with fire."

"I know," he grinned. "Let the morning face-douche commence! In three, two, one..."

He tilted the cup, splashing it all over Lia's face and pillow. She shot up, like a Mentos in a bottle of coke, and gasped. Her mouth was wide open and her eyes were empty, still trying to find their way back from her dream world.

I watched them quickly fill, becoming fully aware of what had just happened. Her eyes then narrowed in on Jeremy and the empty glass in his hand.

"You. Are. *Dead*!" She bellowed. Her face was dripping wet.

Before she could get up, Jeremy dropped the glass and sprinted out the door. I could hear his loud laughter, and then his door slam.

Lia, enraged, roared as she chased after him.

"You will die before this day is over, Jeremy Needles. Do you hear me?" She marched back into my room, and I stood silent. She grabbed her pillow then glanced up to me, and without any emotion she said, "Good morning."

"Good morning. I swear. I had nothing to do with that."

She shook her head. "Do you know if we are sitting next to the exit door on the plane?"

"I'm not sure?" I shrugged.

"If we are, I'm going to pop that hatch and throw him out, preferably somewhere remote." She then turned and walked out.

I laughed, because this was the norm.

Jeremy and Lia packed their things and brought their luggage down to the bottom of the stairs, then we all headed to the kitchen for breakfast.

Miss Lilly had another buffet set up with bacon, eggs, hash browns, pancakes, and an assortment of fruit and cereal. When we entered, Kade, Malachi, and Dominic were already seated and eating. Kade's eyes sparkled as soon as they fixed on me.

"Good morning, Sunshine," he smiled.

"Good morning," I returned, smiling back.

"So, you both leaving us today?" Dominic asked.

"Yes," Lia sighed. "But I will remember this visit forever. It was the best vacation of my life."

"It was the *only* vacation of your life," Jeremy noted.

"It's still the best." Lia shot him a glare.

"So...looks like you and our Caleb here have hooked up,"

Dominic blurted, pointing to Caleb with his fork.

"Yeah, so I'll be back," she said, turning to Caleb with a silly smile.

He blushed and then took a bite of his pancake.

"Ah, young love," Dominic chuckled. Malachi elbowed him.

We all sat around the table, laughing and joking, but it was bittersweet. The proverbial pink elephant was lingering; they would be gone soon. As much as I hated goodbyes Lia hated them more. So I began to mentally prepare myself for lots of messy tears.

After breakfast, we all walked out to the hall. They were leaving in twenty minutes, and my heart and stomach started to twist.

Stop. Be strong. Don't cry. You'll see them again. I repeated this mantra over and over, trying to put my head in the right place.

Alaine stepped into the hallway dressed in a lavender pantsuit, with her hair pulled up into a tight bun.

"Thank you, Lia and Jeremy, for coming and spending some time with us. It has been nothing but joy to have you, and you will always be welcomed here." She hugged them tightly.

"Thank you for having us. We really had a wonderful time, and you have a very beautiful home," Lia said.

"Yes, thank you," Jeremy added. "We both had a great time."

Malachi and Dominic grabbed their luggage and carried it out, and we followed. I grabbed onto Kade's hand.

When we exited, the Hummer was already parked out front. As Courtney and Caleb jumped in, my mantra flew out the window, and my emotions went haywire.

Jeremy stepped forward and hugged me.

"It was great seeing you again, Emma. If you ever need us, you know where we'll be," he said, his voice cracking.

"I'll be in touch. I promise." I attempted to not break down.

He nodded and then extended his hand to Kade. "Please take care of my friend."

"I will," Kade promised, shaking his hand. "It was nice to meet you again."

"Same here," Jeremy grinned. He then stepped back, and slid into the car.

Lia stood staring at me with a pained look in her eyes. Her lips were smiling, but her chin was quivering.

"Don't," I begged.

She shook her head and tears poured from her eyes. She ran to me and wrapped her arms around my neck, sobbing. I hugged her tightly, and my emotions burst. I couldn't hold back.

"Darn you, Lia," I sobbed.

"You know how bad I am at saying goodbye," she whimpered.

"Then, let's not say goodbye," I said. I pulled back and wiped the tears from my face. "Let's say, until next time."

"Alright," she said. "Until next time. And you better be ready for me, because next time I'm bringing a lot more luggage."

"Good," I laughed.

"I'm not kidding," she said. She turned to Kade, and wrapped her arms around him, and he hugged her sweetly.

"Take care of my best friend, Kade. I know I've said that before, but she's the only normal friend I have." She said that last part extra loud, making sure Jeremy heard.

Kade chuckled. "I promise," he said.

She took in a deep breath and exhaled. "Well, you two most beautiful people in the world... It's time I go. And, Emma," she said narrowing her swollen eyes on me. "You better keep in touch this time. I swear. Don't make me have to come back here and hunt you down."

"I promise. I'll send you an email as soon as you leave."

"You better. I'll check. You know me."

"I do."

"Good luck with your testing," she said. I almost forgot about the excuse Alaine gave.

"Thank you. I'll need it. See you soon," I said.

"See you soon," she replied.

She slid in the seat and closed the door. I waved until the car pulled out of sight.

And just like that...they were gone.

I turned to Kade and he wrapped his arms around me. "You've still got me," he said.

"I wouldn't know what I'd do if I didn't." He smiled and led me back into the house. The lack of sleep wrapped itself around my head, making me feel dizzy and my eyes heavy.

"Did you sleep well?" Kade asked.

"I didn't sleep at all," I yawned.

"Well, you should, now that you can. Thomas and Alexander want me to go over to the cottage for a bit. The house is protected. James and Alaine are here, and I think Henry returns this afternoon."

"Where was he?" I asked.

"His sister was ill, so he took a vacation and went back to England to take care of her."

"Oh. It'll be good to see him again," I yawned.

Alaine popped out of her office. "You alright Emma?" she asked.

"Yes, I'm going to get some sleep since I haven't had any yet. Kade is going to the cottage."

"Oh, could you take something to Samuel for me?" she asked.

"Of course." He turned to me, "I'll see you later. Sleep sweet." He leaned over and gave me a kiss.

"I will now," I said, heading up the stairs.

In my room, I went over to the window, and pulled the curtains shut, instantly blacking out the sun. As the room went dark, the sadness lingered, so I pulled back the curtain back a couple of inches to let some sun in. It was comforting.

I dropped to my bed, and immediately faded.

TWENTY
THREE

I JUMPED AWAKE TO A loud thumping. I glanced at my clock. I had been asleep for five hours. Sitting up, I and walked over to the window. The sun was beginning to make its descent. I figured I'd get up, or else I would throw my whole sleeping schedule off. I went to the bathroom and washed up.

Dammit. I forgot to email Lia. But I still had a little time, so I clicked on my laptop and finished brushing my hair. While making my bed, I suddenly had a craving for something sweet. After I sent Lia a quick email, letting her know I took a long nap, I decided to head downstairs.

The house was quiet. Kade must have still been over at the cottage with the others.

As I made my way to the kitchen, I smelled something sweet. When I entered, there were plates filled with homemade cookies on the counter, but Miss Lilly wasn't here. She must have been on break. Dinner still wasn't for a few more hours.

I ambled closer, drawn to their scent. Fresh baked, chocolate chip cookies. I took one and bit into it.

It was heaven. Crunchy on the outside, and warm and gooey on the inside. The chocolate melted in my mouth. They were sinful.

One of the plates was wrapped with cellophane and had a note card attached to it, which read: For Ethon.

I wondered if I should deliver it to him. It would be a nice gesture - sort of a peace offering. I felt horrible for the way things ended last night. I knew it wasn't all his fault. The bond had the three of us twisted in knots and on edge. Truth was, if I had bonded to Ethon first, the tables would probably be turned in his favor.

There was no one around I could tell, but the tower was only a few yards away from the house. I doubted Lucian had eyes on this place every second of the day, and Darkling didn't even come out in daylight. Once I made it to the tower, I knew Ethon would be there to protect me anyway.

I carried the warm plate of cookies to the front door, opened it slightly, and peeked out. It looked completely clear. I took in a deep breath of air, and it was fresh and clear. No scent of Fallen at all. I quickly slipped out and ran to the entrance of the tower. Opening the door, I slipped inside. As soon as the door shut I heard a sound which made me freeze. It sounded like painful moans, almost like someone was injured.

227

What the?

I wondered if Ethon was hurt, or maybe it was Bane or Azzah. I was still trying to be certain I was in fact hearing correctly. A distinct sound of rattling chains and moaning came from up the spiraled stairs.

"Ethon?" I called, but there was no response. I cautiously made my way up.

I'd never been inside the tower, and always wondered what it was like. Towers seemed so mysterious and magical, but also ominous. I wasn't protected by the barrier here, so I needed to be extra careful.

Halfway up, the sounds of the chains and painful groans made the hairs on my skin stand erect.

"Ethon?" I yelled up the stairwell. Again, there was no answer.

I heard a loud thumping sound.

Bang! Bang! Bang!

Holy crap. Someone is up there, and they must be hurt.

My gut instinct was to head toward the sound, but I quickly debated whether it would be better to just run away. Ultimately though, if I was hurt, I would want help.

My heart hammered as I ran up the stairs, accidentally dropping the plate of cookies on my way. The sound of the plate shattering sent a shiver up my spine, but I kept going.

At the top of the stairs, I stopped in a large circular room. Floor to ceiling windows framed in a total 360 degree view of the grounds. It was breathtaking. I could see how this would be the perfect place for Guardians to be stationed.

The inside was beautifully decorated in, a somewhat contemporary, red and gold. It was definitely a place one would be comfortable. On one side there was a large flat-screen TV, accompanied by a surround sound system, and a wrap-around couch. Everything was accented in contemporary colors.

Nothing in the room was over waist height, and everything was away from the windows, all to keep the view completely open.

There were spotlights set up at each window, a telescope, and a screen which showed all of the cameras views from around the grounds. Places I never knew they *had* cameras.

I did a quick scan of the room, only to find it completely empty. There were no signs of Ethon or his goons, but there were empty plates stacked on the counter, next to cases of soda.

How could the room be empty? I swear I heard someone.

"Hello?" I called again. "Is anyone here?"

Another loud clunk made me jump. It was from an area behind me, but when I looked, it was empty. I hadn't felt this scared in a long time. My heart was pounding so hard it threatened to leave my chest.

What the hell could be in here and where is it? I stood, silent.

Bang! Bang! Bang!

The floor under my feet shook after each bang, and I screamed. I was standing on a dark gray carpet, and I suddenly realized it was the only thing in the room that looked out of place. It was totally not part of the color scheme. I held my breath, bent over and tugged it out of the way.

A trap door was revealed... I *hated* trap doors. The last time I was lured into one, bad things happened. I was still dealing with the side effects of that whole ordeal.

Was it one of the Fallen? Or a trap? I started second guessing my decision to forge on by myself. I should probably run back down and get help.

Another deep, painful moan echoed from the door, and I knew that whoever it was, they were in a lot of pain.

I had to help.

Sucking in a deep breath, I walked closer. "Hello?"

There was no answer.

Grabbing hold of the handle with one hand, I released the latch with the other.

There was struggle under the door, and I gathered every bit of strength within me to finish opening it. I wanted to run, but something deep inside me wouldn't let me leave. Whatever it was, kept me there, urging me to open the door.

I hurried over and grabbed a small knife on the counter, and held it in my grasp - just in case. I wasn't sure if it would do anything to keep me safe, but I felt better with at least some kind of a weapon in hand.

The Bloodstone amulet around my neck started to give off a dim glow. I knew, from previous encounters, whenever it glowed, danger was near. But this was different. It was very faint and it kept pulsing, on and off. I didn't have a clue what it meant, so I made a calculated assumption. Maybe there was some kind of danger, but it wasn't a great threat. I hoped I was right.

Twisting the knob, I slowly pushed the door open. I gasped and stepped back. Curled up in a fetal position was a large dark figure. A man. He was naked and covered with old and new blood. His feet and hands were bound, his mouth was gagged. There was blood splattered all over the cell's walls, and also pooled on the floor where he laid.

"Hello?" I said softly, noticing his legs were laying in an awkward position.

Oh my God. They were broken.

His head snapped up, and his swollen, bloodshot eyes locked onto mine. A gag crossed his mouth and his nose was broken, flopping loosely to the side. He was moaning, as if he wanted to tell me something.

I carefully stepped down into the box and untied the gag.

"Thank you," he said, coughing and taking in large mouthfuls of air. His dark black hair was streaked with white, so I knew he must have been older.

"Who are you?" I asked, but he didn't answer. "Who did this to you?" I could smell the smoky aroma associated with the Fallen. "Do you work for Lucian?"

He exhaled, closed his eyes, and laid his head back on the floor.

"I am a member of Lucian's Fallen, and was assigned to be a Watcher. I have no intention of harming anyone, especially you. I'm not a warrior."

"Then why are you here?" I asked.

"A dozen of us were ordered to keep watch over this place. We would report back any and all movement. I had been returning from my watch when I was hit from behind. Next I knew, I was gagged, tied up, and tortured for information."

"Who did this?" I asked.

"The one with Lucifer's eyes. They call him Ethon."

"Ethon?" I whispered to myself. My heart twisted and then anguished. Everything in me began to shake. "Ethon did this to you?" I had to hear it again because my mind just couldn't accept the fact he was capable of doing something like this.

"Yes."

"What exactly did he want from you?" I pressed.

"Information. What Lucian knew about you."

"About me?" My mind was spinning.

"Yes," he paused and took a couple of labored breaths. "He seemed particularly upset when he found out about Alaine being your Nephilim mother. They know of the prophecy." He coughed and his eyes rolled back.

I started hyperventilating. This was worse than I could have ever imagined. Now, I would have both Lucian and Lucifer after me. And what side would Ethon take?

"I honestly didn't mean to put you in danger. Ethon has developed cunning ways of torturing information from his captures. You need to leave, and warn the others. You are in grave danger. Lucian will try to get to you before Lucifer does. If he cannot, he said he will kill you. Lucifer will want you alive."

I needed to get out of here, but I wasn't going to leave him here to die. The chains they had bound around him were too tight, and there was no key.

"I need something to help get you free. I need to get you out of here."

"Don't. Get out before they return."

"I won't leave you here to die."

He grabbed my ankle, forcing me to look him in the eye.

"Save yourself. You need to live. You are the one who can end this senseless war, once and for all. Lucian needs to be stopped. He's gone mad. His murderous spree is fueled by revenge, but once he's had it, he will continue. He wants power, and you're the key."

"Lucian has been gathering his army. Once they have assembled, they will strike. You are his end goal. He believes you are the key to him ruling the Otherworlds. Yes, Lucifer may be just as dark and evil, but at least he has a method to his ways."

"Well, I hope they realize I am worthless for the next eight months," I said.

"Which is why he wants to capture you now, while they still can. Because once you transform…you will have an even greater power."

"Look at me, I can't even get you out of here," I said, helpless.

He squeezed my leg a little tighter, and steeled his swollen eyes on mine.

"I'm done for, child. Go now. Save yourself."

I sobbed. I didn't want to leave him, but I knew there was no way I could break the chains, or carry him out of here. Knowing Ethon did this made me sick.

"Hurry. They will be back soon."

"I'm sorry," I cried.

"I've lived a hundred lives. To die now will be setting me free. Now, give me the knife, close the door, and run."

Tears streamed down my face as I took the knife and placed it in his hands.

"I'm sorry," I whispered.

I closed the trap door, bolted it shut, and quickly threw the rug back over it. I turned to run when I saw three figures flying fast toward the tower. I froze as my eyes locked onto Ethon's red gaze.

TWENTY

FOUR

I RAN FOR THE STAIRS, but he was too fast. In seconds, he was at the glass door on top of the tower. I wished my feet could run as fast as my heart was beating. My breath quickened to the point I thought I'd pass out.

"Emma!" he called out. "Emma!"

"Stay away from me," I yelled, my feet started pounding down the stairs.

"What's the matter?" He sounded concerned.

The bottom door suddenly opened and Bane's twisted, angry face stared up at me. He stepped in and closed the door, and started up the stairs.

"Leave me alone!" I screamed.

"Emma, please come back up here and tell me what's wrong. I have promised to never hurt you."

I knew I was trapped, and I didn't want to take my chances with Bane, so I reluctantly made my way back up toward Ethon.

I stood there, shaking.

"What were you doing here?" he asked.

"I came to bring you cookies." My voice trembled.

"You did?" He grinned.

"Yes, but I dropped them down the stairs on the way up."

"Are you okay? Did you fall?" he asked, stepping closer to me.

My pulse started to race.

"Ethon," Azzah called. Ethon turned back, and he gave him a look. "She knows."

Ethon sighed and closed his eyes.

"Emma. Why did you lie to me?" His eyes furrowed with concern.

"About what exactly?" I questioned.

"Alaine…who you really are," he said softly. Stepping forward, he looked like he was going to hold my hands, but decided against it at the last minute.

"I never lied to you. I just didn't tell you. There's a difference. And, believe me, I'm nothing special. Just a simple girl trying to stay alive in a crazy, murderous world."

"All I have wanted to do is protect you, since the moment we touched. How can I do that when you keep such things from me? This information changes *a lot* of things." He was starting to get upset.

236

"Why? Why would it change things? And why the hell do you have that person chained and gagged under the floor, Ethon?" I asked, getting a little emotional.

"He works for Lucian. We found him snooping around the property. He was watching your every move, Emma. We were only trying to protect you." Ethon looked confused as to why I'd be so upset.

"Protect me by *torturing* him?" My voice became shrill near the end.

"He's immortal. He'll heal in a few days."

"Holy crap, Ethon," I exhaled.

I had a hard time trying to wrap my head around torturing someone for information. And by the look of things, he had absolutely no issues with his methods. I suddenly began to wonder why the bond had connected us.

I saw the damage he did to that man, and it was wrong. He beat the man to a bloody mess, and broke both of his legs. I would maybe be a little more understanding if the person tried to kill them, or had intentions of harming anyone, but he was a Watcher. At least that's what he said.

"Emma, listen," Ethon said, hesitating slightly before grabbing my arms. The shock caused me to jump, but I fought the bond. It was trying to subdue my fears, and I needed to keep my mind strong. The facts could not be muted.

"First, I'm sorry about touching you. I'm not trying to control you, the bond is just begging me to calm you down – soothe your soul. Second, my father found out about you, and it wasn't by me, or

Bane, or Azzah. He has a damn network of reliable and not-so-reliable sources. Because you *failed* to tell me the truth, I had to find out for myself. I'm sorry if the method seems brutal, but I needed to know everything before I met with my father. He can't believe I was oblivious to everything going on around me. I needed to have answers to save you, Emma. I told you, before, and I will say it again, you can trust me. I live now for only one reason, to keep you safe and happy. If you would have told me, we wouldn't have resorted to this."

I shook my head. I was so confused. One part of me wanted to trust him; to believe he really wanted to save me, and actually possessed good inside of him. The other part felt Ethon was evil and there was no escaping it. I just had a hard time seeing past the blood and broken bones.

"He's coming." Ethon said, ominously.

"When?" I gasped.

"Right now."

"Shit. Is he going to kill me?" I asked.

"No. Of course not. I would never allow him to harm you," he said, pulling me close.

I fell into his arms, and was comforted - but didn't hug him back. My heart was aching, and my head was turning in a mad whirlwind, tossing and bashing me into confusion. I wasn't ready to see Lucifer. I knew he was coming for a purpose. He wouldn't leave the Underworld to see me if it wasn't something worth his time.

Without my Guardians, I was left with the only other person I knew who could keep me from Lucifer. I had to put trust in him. At this point I had no other choice.

I wrapped my arms around Ethon, resting my head on his chest. His arms wrapped tightly around me, and I instantly felt protected.

"What does he want?" I asked.

"I don't know, Emma. I would tell you if I knew. He wanted us to find a way to bring you, but to my surprise, you were already here and alone. I guess it was fate."

Yeah, and it sucked to be me right now.

There was nothing I could do. If I tried to get away, scream for help, or fight…things would end badly. I didn't want to put any of the others in danger. Especially, Kade. I knew for a fact he would rush to my rescue, and die fighting for me.

I had only been missing for about ten minutes, and everyone thought I was safely in my room. So, everyone should be fine.

Danyel once told me if Lucifer ever found out my past, he would use me as a pawn. But ultimately, if the prophecy was true, I'd be the one with the power. Why should they be able to use me, if I had the power to defeat them?

I'd need to be smart and play his game. I would make him believe I was going along with whatever plans he had.

"Why is he coming here?"

"Because I wasn't *going* to take you away from the barrier, especially with Lucian's swarm out there," he said.

Ethon was still looking out for me, like he said he would. I wondered if it was just a part he was playing, or if he was sincere. Right now, it didn't matter. I'd take his protection anyway I could get it.

Knowing I would be face to face with Lucifer made me feel like I was suffocating. This whole nightmarish dream was never-ending.

I squeezed closer to Ethon and closed my eyes, preparing for the inevitable.

"I'm here. He won't harm you," Ethon whispered. His words brushed past my ears and I held them tightly in my heart. He was my only hope...*again*.

TWENTY FIVE

A FTER A FEW SECONDS, A cold wind started wrapping around us, and smoke started to seep in from the bottom of the door.

"Is that—?" I whispered.

Ethon nodded and then closed his eyes with an aggravated look on his face.

The smoke became heavier, and started to billow upward into a large spiral. Suddenly, from behind – or maybe out of - the smoke, Lucifer stepped forward. His dark crimson eyes landed on me, safely caressed in Ethon's arms. They narrowed, taunting and tormenting, without even speaking a word.

Bane and Azzah bowed and stepped out of the room.

"Emma, dear. It's quite nice to see you again," he said, insincerely.

"The feeling isn't mutual."

"I shall get straight to the point then, no idle chit-chat. His eyes narrowed on mine. "You and your father kept one major detail from me during your quest in the Underworld. I sensed something was counterfactual, especially concerning your mark. You should know by now, you can never deceive the Deceiver."

I pulled my arms from around Ethon and stepped back, separating myself from him. I didn't want to use him as a crutch anymore. I needed to find my own foothold, even if it meant stumbling and falling.

"If we told you the truth, would you have let us leave?" I questioned, trying to steady my voice.

He stepped closer, brushing his goatee between his finger and thumb. "That would have been highly improbable."

"Then do you blame us for doing what we did to survive?"

"Not if it's at my expense," he growled.

I kept my mouth shut. Trying to reason with him was like talking to a steel wall. Cold, hard, and impenetrable. I knew things could get heated and turn deadly, very quickly.

"My son has also made me aware of a flaw with the bond. It seems there is a *hindrance.* This poses a great problem for us, so I've come up with a solution."

"A solution?" I questioned. I knew it would come with a price.

"Yes. With every problem, there is a solution, and I just so happen to have the solution to *this* particular problem."

I glanced at Ethon, and he slowly shook his head like he had no clue of what was going on. But after talking to the Fallen under the floor, I wasn't sure if I believed him.

"It's simple, really. I will set you free, and allow everyone whom you love so dearly, to live. Samuel - your beloved Nephilim mother, Alaine - your Guardian, *and* all the others including the four mortals."

Dammit to hell. He positively knew about Alaine. I tried to keep my cool and steady my trembling limbs, but it was nearly impossible.

"But?" I knew there was a huge *but* coming up, and it terrified me.

"But, I have one condition," his eyes shrewdly looked me over. "When the time comes, you *will* choose Ethon. And until such time, you will not speak to anyone regarding this prearrangement. If you so much as breathe a word to *anyone*, they will die."

"Screw you!" I screamed. The words automatically traveled from my mind and flew out my mouth.

Before I could blink, Lucifer flew at me like a flash, wrapped his powerful hand around my neck and squeezed until my breath seized completely. My feet were suddenly lifted off the floor, dangling helplessly. I tried to fight and loosen the grip of his long, strong fingers, but they were locked, and I couldn't even gasp for air.

A heat, emanating from his hand, burned my neck. The edges of my vision started to blacken as I stole one last glance at my murderer. His glowering eyes burned bright with evil and ill intent, mixed with a twisted excitement and satisfaction.

My life flashed before my eyes as I struggled, suffocating.

I'm sorry. I said to those who truly loved me. I had fought and had expired every ounce of will left in me. I was too weak and powerless to continue. I'd finally accepted my fate and felt my body go limp.

"Father! Stop. You'll kill her!" I could barely hear Ethon's pleading.

I suddenly felt an impact, and shortly after, Lucifer released his grip, tossing me across the room. I hit the ground and tumbled, gasping and coughing, trying to fill my lungs with valuable air.

As I watched through my tear-filled vision, Lucifer threw Ethon to the ground, and placed his knee on his chest. His eyes were burning with anger as he lifted his hand, ready to strike him.

"Father!" Ethon yelled, his arms shielding his face.

Lucifer hesitated, and suddenly snapped from his rage. He pushed himself back, off of his son.

"Look what this bitch is doing, Ethon. She's driving a wedge between us, drawing us apart."

"She's not the one driving the wedge, father," Ethon answered.

"*Everything* I do is for us. Your lack of respect is a disgrace. It's a dagger pushed into the depths of my heart. Don't ever take my leniency as a sign of weakness. I will have no problem showing you where your place is, Ethon," Lucifer roared.

Ethon stood, but didn't say a word. He kept his head down, but I could see the deep crimson of anger burning within his eyes.

Lucifer's attention shifted. His dangerous eyes fixed on me, almost intent on finding a reason to finish what he had started.

I wouldn't give him the pleasure, so I kept quiet, praying for a chance to repay him. More than ever, I desired to survive until my transformation. Revenge and hatred would be the fuel to the fire burning deep within me. I promised myself I would be the hand of vengeance.

"You will learn very quickly not to mess with me, girl. If it wasn't for Ethon, you would already be dead. I will *not* leave here until you completely understand my terms. So, I will go over them once more for your safety, and the safety of the others around you."

"You *will* choose Ethon and seal the bond *before* your transformation, or everyone you love *will* die. Tell anyone about our arrangement, and *they will die*. It's as simple as that. You can never hide anything from me. If you ever feel the urge to cry on someone's shoulder, look them in the eyes and say goodbye, because it will be the last time you see them alive."

"I may not be omnipotent, but I have ways of knowing all. I have secret eyes and ears everywhere, and they will notify me if you've spoken about our deal. It's your choice. But choose wrong, and their blood will be on your hands."

"So, in other words, I have no choice," I stated.

"If that's how you choose to see it," he said, raising his hands out to the side with unconcern.

He had not one ounce of compassion, remorse, or sympathy. His face was rigid and exuded nothing more than pure evil. Now I knew exactly why he was cast from heaven. His charred heart was bereft of any good or moral values; leaving a sick, arrogant, immortal bastard. Being in his presence caused my heart to experience true hatred.

"Just say the two words - I agree - and I will leave this place."

I glanced at Ethon, but his head was bowed. He couldn't even look at me.

My world had come to a screeching halt. Everything I'd ever hoped for vanished. In an instant, I watched my future disintegrate, like grains of sand falling through my fingers. There was no way I would risk the lives of my loved ones. It wasn't even an option.

I sucked in a deep breath. I was literally about to make a deal with the Devil, and would pay for it for the rest of my existence.

But they were worth it. Kade was worth it. And I could rest knowing they'd be safe.

I lifted my head and faced him without fear.

"I agree."

As the words left my mouth, so did my soul.

Ethon's head rose. His brow was furrowed, and I could tell he realized what I was giving up.

He walked over to me and wrapped me in his arms. "I promise to do everything in my power to make you happy," he whispered.

His words offered little comfort, because standing in the background, with a wicked grin on his face was the one who held our strings. He was our puppet master, playing with us to fulfill his own wicked desires. He knew my greatest weakness, and exactly which strings to tug in order to get what he wanted. He played his game too well.

Ethon could make promises, and they may be honest, but they were hollow. We would never live a happy life, as long as Lucifer was alive. We were but slaves to his will.

"There. Now that wasn't so bad, was it?" Lucifer mocked. "I'll be sure to keep my end of the bargain, and will be here when Lucian strikes. You just remember, you must be bonded to Ethon before your transformation."

And that was it. As swiftly as a wisp of wind, Lucifer was gone, leaving behind him a whirlwind of destruction. He needed me to be bonded to Ethon *before* the transformation because he wanted to seal his position of power.

My eyes misted over and a beautiful face with hazel eyes came to mind. Even embraced within the arms of Ethon, I felt hollow. Betrayed. What hurt the most was I would eventually have to break Kade's heart, and he would never know why.

"I'm so sorry, Emma. I didn't want you to be forced into a decision, but we will make the best of it. I promise to love you for the rest of our lives," he whispered. I couldn't help but wonder if Ethon had a hand in this.

A tear escaped and trailed down my cheek. But deep inside, I knew I would never allow the bond to strip my memories from me. I would *never* forget him.

What had started out as a quest to seek help, had quickly backfired. I shouldn't have been surprised. We were dealing with the Deceiver. The Prince of Darkness. He was bound to find out sooner or later.

I quickly realized...I never really had a choice. I was always going to be the Devil's pawn.

I closed my eyes, and then, a spark of awareness flashed through my mind. I had an epiphany. A way to possibly end all of this madness. It was a huge risk, and I wasn't sure if it was even possible, but I was willing to try.

I would play the game, and play it well. I would let him think he had me. But in actuality...he didn't. This was my destiny, and I wouldn't let anyone, including the Devil himself, decide my fate.

I opened my eyes as a new spark of hope ignited within me.

Little did the Devil know...two could play this game.

I was a dark horse.

And I was ready.

ABOUT CAMEO:

Cameo Renae was born in San Francisco, raised in Maui, Hawaii, and recently moved with her husband and children to Alaska.

She's a daydreamer, a caffeine and peppermint addict, loves to laugh, loves to read, and loves to escape reality. One of her greatest joys is creating fantasy worlds filled with adventure and romance, and sharing it with others.

One day she hopes to find her own magic wardrobe, and ride away on her magical unicorn. Until then...she'll keep writing.

WWW.CAMEORENAE.COM

KEEP READING FOR A SNEAK PEEK OF ...

GILDED WINGS

EXCERPT

S ITTING AT THE EDGE OF a small lake, I am dipping my feet
in and out of the crystal clear water; appreciating the magical
weather. The sun is shining, and the sky is the most
unbelievable blue. I was almost like a painting. The large tree behind
me is providing perfect amount of shade. The grass beneath me is
bright green, and feathery soft to the touch.

A few yards away, near the water's edge, two beautiful, children
play. Their dark hair glimmering in the sun. The little boy is being
chased around by the older girl, their laughter filling the air, making
me buzz with delight.

A large, strong hand finds mine and squeezes. Leaning back, I
breathe in the heady scent of my bonded. My soul mate. He is lying
beside me, with one arm behind his head.

"Are the little devils behaving themselves?" he asks.

I turn to face him and use my free hand to draw circles up and down his chest. "Yes. They seem to enjoy this place, almost as much as we do."

"It's a shame we haven't flown here as a family more often." Turning his head, his mesmerizing eyes lock onto mine in earnest. "We'll have to remedy that in the future."

My eyes popped open. I sat up, bewildered, not knowing if what I had just experienced was a dream, or a premonition. Whatever it was seemed so real. I rested my hand to my heart, and took a slow, steadying breath.

It couldn't be real…could it?